"I don't believe... afraid that somehow I'll fall for you."

Marissa threw back her head and laughed.

"I don't see what's so damned funny," Jack answered indignantly.

She stepped close to him and placed a hand on his arm. "Trust me, Jack. You have nothing to worry about. You are nothing like the man I intend to marry. At this point, I'm not even sure I like you very much." Still laughing, she picked up her son and left the balcony.

Jack stared after her, wondering why it irritated him that a woman he hadn't even known before two days ago was so certain she could never, ever fall for him....

Dear Reader,

Although the anniversary is over, Silhouette Romance is still celebrating our coming of age—we'll soon be twenty-one! Be sure to join us each and every month for six emotional stories about the romantic journey from first time to forever.

And this month we've got a special Valentine's treat for you! Three stories deal with the special holiday for true lovers. Karen Rose Smith gives us a man who asks an old friend to *Be My Bride?* Teresa Southwick's latest title, *Secret Ingredient: Love,* brings back the delightful Marchetti family. And Carla Cassidy's *Just One Kiss* shows how a confirmed bachelor is brought to his knees by a special woman.

Amusing, emotional and oh-so-captivating Carolyn Zane is at it again! Her latest BRUBAKER BRIDES story, *Tex's Exasperating Heiress,* features a determined groom, a captivating heiress and the pig that brought them together. And popular author Arlene James tells of *The Mesmerizing Mr. Carlyle,* part of our AN OLDER MAN thematic miniseries. Readers will love the overwhelming attraction between this couple! Finally, *The Runaway Princess* marks Patricia Forsythe's debut in the Romance line. But Patricia is no stranger to love stories, having written many as Patricia Knoll!

Next month, look for appealing stories by Raye Morgan, Susan Meier, Valerie Parv and other exciting authors. And be sure to return in March for a new installment of the popular ROYALLY WED tales!

Happy reading!

Mary-Theresa Hussey

Mary-Theresa Hussey
Senior Editor

Please address questions and book requests to:
Silhouette Reader Service
U.S.: 3010 Walden Ave., P.O. Box 1325, Buffalo, NY 14269
Canadian: P.O. Box 609, Fort Erie, Ont. L2A 5X3

Just One Kiss

CARLA CASSIDY

SILHOUETTE *Romance*

Published by Silhouette Books

America's Publisher of Contemporary Romance

SILHOUETTE BOOKS

ISBN 0-373-19496-X

JUST ONE KISS

Copyright © 2001 by Carla Bracale

This edition published by arrangement with Harlequin Books S.A.

Visit Silhouette at www.eHarlequin.com

Printed in U.S.A.

Books by Carla Cassidy

CARLA CASSIDY

is an award-winning author who has written over thirty-five books for Silhouette. In 1995 she won Best Silhouette Romance from *Romantic Times Magazine* for *Anything for Danny*. In 1998 she also won a Career Achievement Award for Best Innovative Series from *Romantic Times Magazine*.

Carla believes the only thing better than curling up with a good book to read is sitting down at the computer with a good story to write. She's looking forward to writing many more books and bringing hours of pleasure to readers.

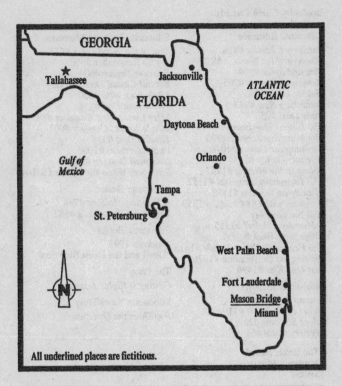

GEORGIA

★ Tallahassee

Jacksonville

FLORIDA

ATLANTIC OCEAN

Daytona Beach

Orlando

Gulf of Mexico

Tampa

St. Petersburg

West Palm Beach

Fort Lauderdale

Mason Bridge

Miami

N

All underlined places are fictitious.

Prologue

"Aren't they cute?" Samantha Curell pointed to the three toddlers playing in the day-care sandbox.

Samantha's assistant, Marie, nodded. "They always play well together. And the way they chatter, it's as if their gibberish is their very own language and they're solving the world's problems."

Actually the three toddlers were not solving the world's problems. Instead, the two little girls were bragging to the little boy.

"My daddy took me to the movies last night," eighteen-month-old Claire boasted in the toddler language only other toddlers understood.

"So what?" Twenty-month-old Julie looked bored. "My daddy bought me a new doll and it hugs me when I squeeze its tummy."

Both girls looked at two-year-old Nathaniel. He frowned. Sometimes he didn't like girls at all, especially girls who had daddies and liked to brag.

He shoved a toy truck along the floor, trying to pretend he didn't care about the fact that he didn't have a father.

"My daddy is so strong, sometimes he lifts me up to touch the ceiling," Claire continued.

"Well, my daddy is a policeman and he arrests bad people, so he's *really* strong," Julie said, refusing to be outdone.

Unable to resist, Nathaniel abandoned the toy truck. "I'm gonna get me a daddy and he'll be the best daddy in the whole wide world."

Claire laughed, her blue eyes disbelieving. At that moment Nathaniel decided that when he got married, he'd marry a woman with brown eyes. "Where are you going to get a daddy?" she asked.

"On vacation. My mom is taking me on a trip tomorrow. A vacation trip. When I get back, I'm gonna have a dad."

"How are you gonna do that?" Julie asked.

Nathaniel frowned. "I'm not sure, but I'll think of something."

"I'll believe it when I see it," Claire replied, her little nose in the air.

"You wait and see, I'm going to get me a great daddy," Nathaniel vowed. He turned at the sound of his mother's voice.

Marissa Criswell stood talking to Miss Samantha.

They were talking grown-up talk and Nathaniel didn't understand all the words. Just as the grown-ups didn't understand when he talked to his friends.

"I gotta go," Nathaniel said to the girls. He carefully climbed out of the sandbox. "I'll see you when I get back and then you'll see the daddy I bring home."

Nathaniel ran to his mom, who opened her arms to welcome him. "Hi, sweetheart," Marissa said as she picked him up and kissed his cheek. "Were you a good boy today?" Nathaniel snuggled against his mother, who always smelled so nice.

Marissa smiled at Miss Samantha. "Okay, then we'll see you when we get back."

"Have a wonderful time," Miss Samantha replied. "Bye-bye, Nathaniel." She wiggled her fingers and Nathaniel waved back.

As Marissa carried Nathaniel to their car parked in front of the Hickory Dickory Day Care, Nathaniel gave her neck an extra squeeze.

He knew she had no idea what he had planned. But a boy shouldn't grow up without a dad. One way or another he was going to get one. And if he got himself a dad, that meant he'd be getting his mom a man—whether she liked it or not!

Excitement made him wiggle impatiently as his mom buckled him into his car seat. Oh, yes, he had a mission...and that mission was to get a daddy.

Chapter One

Sinful.

Decadent.

These words fluttered through Marissa Criswell's mind as she stretched languidly against the sun-warmed towel. Mason Bridge Beach, Florida, in late June. Three glorious weeks of sun and sand. Three glorious weeks of no work and all play.

She cracked open one eye and raised her head to check on her son. He sat at her feet, shoveling sand across her toes. His blond hair glistened in the sunlight, and his little features were somber with concentration.

Love swelled in her heart and she sent a small prayer heavenward, a prayer of thanks that her grandmother had gifted her with this vacation. Three weeks of quality time with her son—that was the best thing of all. No hospital for her, no day care for him.

In the distance she could see the ocean waves, see the growing crowd setting up umbrellas and blankets between the water and her and Nathaniel's spot. It was still early, but before long the beach would be filled with people seeking relief from the heat with a day at the waterfront.

She rested her head back down and sighed with pleasure. This was the first vacation she'd had in years. Even when she'd been pregnant, she'd worked until the day before delivery, then had gone back to work two weeks after Nathaniel was born.

Her grandmother had made all the arrangements. She'd arranged for Marissa to have the time off from the hospital, gotten the plane tickets and the motel room, then had presented Marissa with a fait accompli. It was the absolute best present Marissa had ever received in her entire life.

Realizing she no longer felt Nathaniel spooning sand across her feet, she once again opened her eyes and lifted her head. "Nathaniel," she called to the little boy, who now sat about fifty feet away from her. "Come back here, sweetie," she said.

Nathaniel didn't acknowledge her, but rather stood and walked several more feet away, then plopped down in the sand once again.

"Nathaniel!" Reluctantly Marissa pulled herself

up and off the blanket, pausing a moment to swipe sand from her body.

When she looked back at her son, a cry choked in her throat. In a single instant she saw the runner, a man clad only in a pair of jogging pants, racing hell-bent for leather and apparently not seeing the fair-haired child in his path.

Marissa's scream ripped from her throat, piercing the calm of the morning. At the same moment the jogger apparently saw Nathaniel. He attempted to veer, but the maneuver went awry when Nathaniel stood and appeared to grab at the man's legs.

As if in slow motion, the man fell and Marissa heard the sickening snap of a bone breaking, then the hard whack of his hand connecting with a piece of driftwood. He yelled, the hoarse roar of agonizing pain.

Nathaniel pointed to the prone man and grinned.

"Oh, dear God." Marissa raced to where the man lay, his right leg at an awkward angle that could only mean a break. "Somebody call 911," she cried to the crowd, then crouched next to the man, who was attempting to sit up. "Lie still," she said. "Help is on the way."

His eyes were a startling blue against his dark tan. Ebony whiskers covered his cheeks and chin and, coupled with his wild, thick hair, gave him the fierce look of a man on the edge. She couldn't be sure if it was pain or anger that glittered in his eyes, made the blue look icy cold and hard as nails.

"That kid tried to kill me," he said between clenched teeth.

Anger, Marissa decided. Definitely anger. "I'm sorry. I'm so sorry." As she looked at the hand that had hit the driftwood, she suspected he had a couple of broken fingers as well as the broken leg.

Guilt tore through her. It was her fault. All her fault. She should have been watching Nathaniel more closely. "I can't tell you how sorry I am," she exclaimed.

"What are you sorry for?" he asked, his forehead wrinkled into a grimace of pain.

"It was my kid...my son."

"What do you call him? The terminator?" he growled.

Marissa flushed, and knelt down. He roared again and she realized her knee was planted on his good hand. "Oh, I'm sorry." She moved her knee off his hand and accidentally hit him in the ribs.

"Jeez, lady, just move back before you kill me," he snarled.

Any further conversation was cut short as paramedics arrived on the scene. They loaded the man onto a stretcher and headed back toward the waiting ambulance.

Marissa grabbed her things, picked up Nathaniel and hurried after them. Moments later, in her rental car, she followed the ambulance to the local hospital.

"I can't believe this is happening," she muttered

to herself as she tailed the big white vehicle. How had the morning that had started off so wonderful suddenly gone so wrong? At least they weren't using a siren, which meant his injuries weren't life threatening.

Nathaniel seemed completely unconcerned about the chaos he'd created. He jabbered to himself, smiling as if amused by the entire scene.

Marissa wasn't amused. She was scared. What if it was worse than a broken leg? Although a broken leg was certainly bad enough! What if he decided to sue her? If push came to shove, he could probably take her for everything she was worth.

She smiled ruefully at this thought. Everything she owned wouldn't add up to a hill of beans. She had a little over two hundred dollars in a Christmas fund account and maybe a hundred dollars in coins in Nathaniel's piggy bank. She didn't own a house and would be lucky if her old clunker car lasted another thousand miles.

Her rueful smile faded as she thought of his injuries. What if the man was a marathon runner training for the Olympics? It would be impossible for him to continue his training with a cast on his leg.

Or maybe he was a bouncer at one of the many local nightclubs in the area, she speculated as she thought of his broad shoulders. How would he tell people that he'd been annihilated by a two-year-old?

With a broken leg and broken fingers, no matter

what he did for a living, he'd be more than inconvenienced by his injuries. He'd be incapacitated.

Guilt once again ripped through her. If only she'd been watching Nathaniel more carefully. If only she hadn't closed her eyes, even for a brief moment.

The ambulance pulled into the emergency entrance of the hospital and Marissa quickly parked in the visitors' lot. She paused only long enough to put on her bathing suit cover-up, then she grabbed Nathaniel and hurried into the hospital.

She was just in time to see the man being wheeled through the double doors and into what she assumed was an examination room.

Surprisingly, the waiting room was empty. She held Nathaniel in her lap and sank onto one of the plastic chairs. She wasn't sure what she intended to do, but she had to make sure the man was okay, had to extend her apologies once again for the freak accident that had occurred.

She knew she should offer to pay his medical bills, and her heart sank at the very thought. She knew how expensive the bill would probably be. Emergency-room treatment never came cheap.

She'd have to somehow borrow the money. She hated to have to go to her grandmother, who had already been more than generous in giving her this vacation.

Rubbing a hand across her forehead, she tried not to think of what another bill would do to her financial status. As a single parent, she found finances were always a source of mild panic.

Sighing, she hugged Nathaniel and reminded herself that somehow she'd figure out some way to make things right with the man her son had mangled.

Jack Coffey grimaced as Dr. Edmund Hall splinted and wrapped the four broken fingers of his right hand. His leg was already encased in a plaster cast up to midthigh. He couldn't believe this was happening. As usual, fate had given him a swift kick in the butt. He should be getting used to it by now.

"So, are you going to tell me how this happened?" Edmund asked as he finished up with Jack's fingers.

"You wouldn't believe me if I told you," Jack said dryly.

Edmund smiled. "You'd be surprised what I'd believe when it comes to you." The two men had been friends for years. "Let me guess," Edmund continued. "You were tailing some wicked wife for a client and she spied you and beat the heck out of you with her purse."

Jack scowled. "Not even close."

"Okay, you were drunk and didn't remember that there's a set of steps outside your house."

"I don't get drunk," Jack countered.

Edmund snorted with disbelief. "You rarely stay sober."

"A lot you know," Jack returned irritably. "I've been clean and sober for the past year. And if you must know, I was jogging on the beach when this kid grabbed my legs. I fell and there was this piece of driftwood and here I am."

"How old was the kid?"

Jack shrugged, then grimaced, realizing there wasn't a place on his body that didn't ache from the jarring fall. "He was a big kid…maybe five or six." He felt heat rise to his cheeks.

He couldn't very well tell Edmund that the kid had been no bigger than a peanut. "Are we done here?"

Edmund nodded. "You want a prescription for some pain pills?"

"No."

"Jack, there's no need to be a tough guy. You're going to hurt."

"I'll be fine," Jack replied, although his leg and fingers throbbed and every muscle he possessed ached, as well.

"You're a stubborn cuss, Jack Coffey." Edmund sighed. "I put on a walking cast, but you're going to need crutches for the first few days. Let me get you a set, then you can be on your way." Edmund left the small examining room.

Jack stared down at the cast on his leg. Terrific. This was just terrific. He had more cases to work now than ever in the history of his private investigative service. How could he stay inconspicuous with this enormous white elephant on his leg?

The entire accident had been weird. He would swear that the kid had actually grabbed his leg, as if meaning to intentionally trip him up.

A vision of the kid's mother filled his head. Horrified green eyes, a cloud of blond curls and a trim little body in a blue bikini, she'd looked like an angel. And had a demon seed for a son, he thought irritably.

"Here we are." Edmund returned with a set of crutches and handed them to Jack. "Want me to show you how to use those?"

"I think I can figure them out," Jack replied with a touch of sarcasm. How hard could it be to use crutches?

"You know, you might want to get somebody to help you out, for a few days at least. Mobility is difficult with a broken leg. And you're going to find that being one-handed is fairly difficult, as well. Is Maria still cleaning house for you?"

"Yeah, why?" The two men left the examining room, Jack stumbling slightly as he tried to get the hang of walking on two wooden sticks instead of two legs.

"Maybe you could get her to stay for a couple of days, make sure you're surviving all right."

"No way," Jack replied. "Maria thinks I'm the devil incarnate. She only cleans for me because I pay her an obscene amount and she only does what she feels like doing. Besides, I don't like her."

Edmund laughed. "You don't like anyone." He grabbed his pager from his coat pocket. "I've got a call." He clapped Jack on the back. "Make an appointment at my office in a couple of days and let me check you out." Without waiting for a reply, Edmund turned and hurried down the hall back to the examining rooms.

Jack watched him go, then leaned for a moment against the wall. With every minute that passed, the pain in his leg and hand was increasing. He drew a deep breath, placed the pads of the crutches beneath his arms, then attempted to shove through the double doors that led to the exit.

He swallowed a mouthful of curses as it took him three tries to open the door and slide through.

He stopped short as he spied the woman and her kid. She rose at the sight of him and the little boy clapped his hands. Her eyes widened as she saw the cast on his leg, his bandaged hand and the areas of his shoulders where the sand had scraped him raw.

"What are you doing here?" he demanded. As if she and her child hadn't already done enough damage. The kid had downed him, then she'd moved in for the kill.

"I came to see what I can do to help. I'm so sorry about all this. Surely there's something I can do...maybe pay your medical bills?" She winced, as if afraid he might agree to her offer.

"I've got insurance," he said gruffly. Besides, she didn't look as if she could afford to buy him a cup of water. Her sandals were old and worn, and the bathing suit cover-up she wore was faded from a multitude of washings.

She didn't appear to be the typical tourist who occasionally stumbled upon the charm of the small town, strutting the beach in the latest finery, flashing diamonds that would feed a family of four for months.

Part of him assessed her as a private investigator would. The other part of him assessed her as a man. Her hair looked soft as silk and framed her delicate features. The cover-up did little to hide her lush curves. She was pretty, and looking at her made a strange ball of heat fire up in the pit of his stomach. That irritated him. At the moment, everything irritated him.

"Please...there must be something I can do to make this right, Mr. Coffey."

He frowned. "How do you know my name?"

"One of the nurses told me." She shifted the boy from one hip to the other. "I feel one hundred percent responsible for your injuries. You must let me do something to make this right."

Anger welled up inside Jack. "Lady, you can't make this right. If you'd been watching your kid, this would have never happened." He took several awkward steps toward the outer door, aggravated as she hurriedly grabbed the door handle and yanked it open for him. He yelped as the door hit his good leg.

"Oh, I'm sorry." She gasped in horror.

Jack shook his head, momentarily afraid to speak, and stepped out into the bright sunshine, the woman and her kid right next to him. "I've got a dozen reports to type up, which will be fun since I only have one working hand. I'm in the middle of cases that require me to be mobile. There's nothing you can do to make this right unless you can lay hands on me and heal me instantly." Each word shot out of him like a bullet into a bull's-eye.

"I can type."

He turned to glare at her and, unwavering, she held his gaze. "Good for you." He hobbled down the sidewalk away from her.

"I could type up your reports." Once again she fell into step beside him. She smelled pretty, like a sun-drenched flower, and again he felt a flutter of heat in the pit of his stomach.

"I don't want you typing up my reports. You'd probably crash my computer."

"How are you getting home?"

The question made him stop in his tracks. He'd been walking to get away from her, but now he contemplated her words. He'd jogged to the beach from his house, but there was no way he could now jog back. "I'll call for a cab."

"That's ridiculous," she replied. "I've got a car right here. I can take you home. Please." She placed a hand on his arm, her eyes luminous with need. "Let me at least do that much for you."

Suddenly Jack was too tired, too much in pain to argue. All he wanted to do was get home and put his aching body to bed. "Okay," he agreed, then frowned at the boy in her arms. "As long as you keep that monster away from me for the duration of the drive."

Her cheeks flushed a pretty pink and her arms tightened around the child. "He's not a monster. He's really a very good little boy."

"Yeah, I hear that's what they used to say about the Unabomber," Jack retorted dryly.

Her blush deepened, and this time he thought it might be anger that colored her cheeks. She drew an audible breath, then pointed to the parking lot. "My car is over there. I'll just go get it."

Jack nodded and leaned wearily against the building, wondering if she could manage to get him home without any major catastrophes. He couldn't help but feel a horrifying sense of impending doom.

Chapter Two

It took Marissa several minutes to rearrange the car to make room for Jack. She quickly moved the diaper bag to the floor at Nathaniel's feet in the backseat. She then pushed the passenger seat back as far as it would go and reclined it. Jack Coffey was tall, and she knew he'd need as much leg room as he could get.

A moment later she pulled up against the curb where he stood waiting for her. She jumped out of the car to help him, but he waved her away. "Just take these," he said as he held out the crutches. "I'd prefer to get into the car without your help. It's safer."

He eased down onto the seat, then groaned as he lifted the cast-encased leg into the car. Marissa placed the crutches between them, then got in behind the steering wheel.

"Are you okay?" she asked worriedly. Even with a scowl cutting into his forehead, the man was handsome as sin. His scent filled the interior of the car, a bold, masculine smell that was at once both attractive and disturbing.

"Just get me home," he replied. His seat was reclined so far back, his head was almost even with Nathaniel. "He's buckled in real tight, isn't he?"

"Of course," Marissa replied as she put the car into gear. "You'll have to tell me how to get to your house."

"Go out the hospital exit and turn left." He closed his eyes.

"By the way, my name is Marissa. Marissa Criswell. And that big guy in the backseat is my son, Nathaniel."

"I prefer to think of you and your son as my own personal nightmare," he returned without opening his eyes.

Marissa flushed, but reminded herself that his rudeness was warranted and probably intensified by the fact that he was in pain. "Do you have a wife? Somebody who can take care of you?" she asked.

His eyes opened. "A wife would be my other personal nightmare. I've been by myself for the last five years and that's the way I like it. Just get me home and I'll be fine."

So, he had no wife and apparently no significant

other. Marissa frowned, wondering if he had any real concept of how a broken leg and a few broken fingers could complicate even the simplest things in life.

"You mentioned you have reports to type and cases to take care of. What kind of work do you do, Mr. Coffey?" she asked to break the stifling silence.

"I'm a ballet dancer. Think I'll be able to get tights over this baby?" He banged the cast with the back of his good hand.

"You don't have to get sarcastic," she said softly.

He frowned and rubbed a hand across his forehead. "I'm a private investigator."

"Really? Are you any good?"

His eyes glittered and a small smile curved the corners of his lips. Marissa felt the power of his devastating smile right down to her toes. She tightened her hands on the steering wheel and tried to ignore how that smile of his affected her on a distinctly female level.

"I'm the best," he said. In the blink of his eye, the smile disappeared, replaced by a scowl so menacing, Marissa decided to let the subject drop.

For the next few minutes he spoke only to give her directions. As he pointed her down a narrow road with tall trees and heavy vegetation on either side, a small flutter of anxiety whispered through Marissa. She could see no houses, no indication of civilization anywhere. They passed a tree with a sign reading No Trespassers.

Was it possible he was bringing her out in the woods to strangle her? She knew nothing about him other than his name. Maybe he intended to break her leg, just to teach her a lesson or vent his ire.

She cast him a quick glance, then relaxed. She could outrun him. Even with Nathaniel in her arms, she knew she could run faster than an angry maniac with a cast. Besides, his face was sickly pale and he looked as if just getting out of the car would provide challenge enough.

The woodland on either side of the road disappeared and suddenly they were on what appeared to be a sheltered private beach, the ocean a huge expanse of blue on their left.

Jack pointed to the single house on the right, a glass-fronted structure that seemed to be clinging to the hillside. "That's it."

Marissa parked the car, slid out and grabbed the crutches, then hurried around to the passenger side to help him out.

"I'd like to say it's been a pleasure, but it hasn't," he said as he situated the crutch pads beneath his arms. He started toward the house, then paused, looking up at the set of steep stairs that led to the door.

"I'd better help you," Marissa said. She checked Nathaniel, who was safely buckled in, then moved to Jack's side and took one of his crutches. "You can lean on me, and that will make it easier."

He hesitated a moment, obviously reluctant to accept her offer.

"Or you can do it yourself and risk the possibility of falling, in which case you'll have nobody to blame but yourself," she said with a touch of impatience.

"And if I fall with you helping me, then I get to blame you?"

"Exactly," she replied dryly. He nodded and wrapped an arm around her shoulder. She placed a hand on his back to steady him. His skin was pleasantly warm, and as he leaned into her she smelled the faint scent of a spicy cologne.

It had been a very long time since she'd been this close to a man who was so overwhelmingly masculine. Despite her concern about him, pleasure winged through her at the tactile contact between her hand and his broad, muscled back.

"Aren't you afraid Baby-Face Nelson will steal the car while you're helping me?" he asked gruffly as they carefully maneuvered the first two steps.

"Don't be ridiculous," she scoffed. "Nathaniel is just barely two, and he's certainly not a hardened criminal." They went up two more stairs.

"Ah, the mother is always the last to admit there's a problem."

Marissa halted their forward progress. "Mr. Coffey, you don't strike me as a stupid man. But it's incredibly stupid to malign a woman's child when said woman is helping you up a very steep set of stairs.''

He turned and looked at her in surprise. ''Touché.'' The hint of a grudging smile glittered in his eyes. Marissa's breath caught in her chest.

She had a feeling that beneath the scratchy whiskers and without the lines of pain that tightened his features, Jack Coffey had the kind of face that could steal more than a heart.

With the curve of his lips, he could make a woman think of silky sheets and hot nights and arms and legs tangled in desire. She frowned, wondering if perhaps she'd suffered a touch of sunstroke. Surely that was the only explanation for her crazy, out-of-character thoughts.

Once again they continued the arduous climb up the remainder of the stairs. When they reached the top, Marissa handed him back his crutch and released her hold on him. ''Are you sure you're going to be all right?'' she asked worriedly.

Once again his face was unnaturally pale and a light sheen of perspiration shone on his forehead. ''I told you, I'll be fine.'' He turned and entered the house and shut the door in her face.

Marissa fought the impulse to bang on the door and tell him he was a rude jerk. Instead she reminded herself that pain often made people extremely ill-tempered.

As a nurse's aide, she'd seen pain transform rational, intelligent, nice people into cursing, screaming creatures who hardly resembled human beings.

She turned, went down the stairs and got back into the car, smiling at her son in the rearview mirror. "Well, sweetie, I offered to help him, but he declined. I guess that's the end of our responsibility."

Nathaniel laughed, the childish giggle that always wound itself around Marissa's heart. As she started the car and drove away from Jack Coffey's place, she wondered if Bill ever thought of her, ever wondered about his son. She wondered if he realized how much he'd given up when he'd chosen to walk away from them both.

As she drove to the motel that she and Nathaniel were calling home for the duration of their vacation, she filed thoughts of Bill away.

She hadn't realized at the time they were dating just how immature and selfish he was. She hadn't realized that until she'd gotten pregnant and he'd run for the hills. She didn't need a scared boy in her life, and Nathaniel certainly didn't need a scared boy for a father.

Better to have no father figure in Nathaniel's life than a bad one. She'd grown up with a father who'd been immature and unwilling to accept responsibility.

He'd drifted in and out of her life on his whims, bearing expensive gifts she didn't need, taking her to restaurants she didn't care about, giving her tangible things when all she wanted and needed was his love.

He'd been filed away with Bill in her "not worth thinking about" file. And now she had a third man to add. Jack Coffey.

But Jack simply refused to stay filed away. As she and Nathaniel ate dinner in a restaurant near her motel room, she wondered what Jack was eating for supper. With his splinted and bandaged hand, even making a sandwich could prove difficult.

Not my problem, she reminded herself. She'd offered to help and he'd declined. From her brief encounter with him, she had a feeling Jack Coffey was a man who would have difficulty asking for help under any circumstances.

Much later, tucked into bed with Nathaniel sleeping next to her in the crib the motel had provided, the scent of his baby sweetness surrounding her, she once again worried about Jack.

She couldn't help feeling responsible for him and his injuries. What if he tried to maneuver down those steep stairs on his own? As isolated as his house was, he could fall and hurt himself badly and it might be days before anyone would find him.

When she finally fell asleep, her dreams were nightmares of Jack Coffey chasing her down the beach, only in her dreams it was her leg that was encased in heavy plaster. Nathaniel sat on the sand, clapping his hands and laughing with glee each time Jack tried to grab her.

She awoke with a start just after dawn, grateful to leave the nightmares behind. But the night of restless dreams had made her realize she couldn't just go on her merry vacation knowing a man was suffering because of her and her son's actions. Her conscience simply wouldn't allow it.

By eight, she and Nathaniel were dressed and on their way back to Jack's house. In a sack in the backseat she had all the makings of a good, old-fashioned, home-cooked breakfast. She didn't know a man alive who would say no to biscuits and gravy, thick slabs of ham and fresh eggs.

When she pulled up outside Jack's house, she was surprised to see an old, beat-up station wagon. She sat for a moment, wondering if she should go up or not. After all, the station wagon indicated he wasn't alone.

As she was trying to make up her mind what to do, the front door flew open and an older, heavyset, gray-haired woman exited. She went halfway down the stairs, then turned back as Jack appeared in the doorway.

"Don't come back, Maria. You're fired!" Jack bellowed, causing several seagulls who'd been walking the beach to squawk and take flight.

"Okay." Maria nodded and smiled. "I'm fired." She continued down the stairs as Jack slammed the door. As Maria hurried to the station wagon, she offered Marissa a wide grin. "Be careful. He's very cranky this morning."

"Thanks," Marissa replied, surprised by the woman's friendliness. She got Nathaniel from his car seat, grabbed the sack of groceries and the diaper bag, then stared up the staircase. "Very cranky," she repeated beneath her breath. "He wasn't exactly Mr. Sunshine yesterday. How much worse can it be?"

She climbed the stairs and set the sack of groceries down, then knocked on the door.

"Go away." Jack's voice came from somewhere inside the house. "I said you were fired."

Marissa drew a deep breath, then cracked open the door. "Mr. Coffey? It's me, Marissa." The door jerked out of her hand and she found herself face-to-face with the man himself.

"What in the hell are you doing here?"

It was apparent that he'd had a rough night. His hair stood askew and the stubble that darkened his cheeks and chin was thicker. His eyes were midnight-blue, with dark, bruiselike circles beneath. His appearance provoked a renewed burst of heartfelt guilt to seep through Marissa.

"I've come to make you some breakfast," she said. He stared at her as if she'd lost her mind. She grabbed the sack. "I—I brought everything I need."

Nathaniel wiggled in her arms and pointed to Jack, who scowled irritably. "What did you bring?" he asked grudgingly.

"Ham and eggs, biscuits and milk to make gravy."

He hesitated a moment, then stumbled away from the door. "Knock yourself out."

Marissa entered the house and caught her breath. The first thing that stole her breath away was the view. The living room had one wall of glass, offering a splendid panorama of the beach and the ocean.

The second thing that made her catch her breath was the utter chaos that reigned in the room. The surface of the coffee table was covered with old newspapers, empty soda cans and a variety of fast-food wrappers.

The computer workstation in one corner of the room appeared to be an extension of the coffee table. More fast-food wrappers, empty cans and bottles of juice and stacks of paperwork covered the entire area. The carpeting needed vacuuming and what little wood she saw needed polishing.

"Don't mind the mess," he said as he sank onto the sofa where a bed pillow and a blanket awaited him. "I just fired my housekeeper."

"I think I met her on the way in," Marissa replied.

"She was supposed to work for me today, but stopped by to tell me there was an important bingo game and her sister the psychic told her today was her lucky day."

"I wouldn't consider getting fired particularly lucky," Marissa exclaimed. "But she didn't look too upset about losing her job."

Jack sighed and raked a hand through his hair.

"Hell no, she wasn't upset. She intentionally aggravates me so I'll fire her because she knows I'll call her to come back and she'll decline and I'll offer her a raise and she'll come back."

He might be cranky, but at least he was more talkative this morning than he'd been yesterday, Marissa thought.

"I see you brought the death squad with you," he said. "Don't you have a husband to watch him while you pursue your mission of mercy?"

"No, I don't." Marissa wasn't about to get into a conversation about her personal life. She decided to take immediate control of the situation. "Why don't you just lie down and rest and I'll have a good breakfast for you in a little while."

He nodded, eased himself into a prone position, then pointed to the doorway behind her. "The kitchen is that way."

Marissa stifled a groan of dismay as she entered the kitchen. Although it was a large, homey room, at the moment it was a little too homey. The sink was filled with dirty dishes and the counters were cluttered with the leftovers of several meals.

The man was a pig, Marissa thought. This mess wasn't the result of a man with a broken leg and fingers trying to feed himself. This mess hadn't made itself in the past twenty-four hours. It had taken at least three to four days to achieve this maximum sloppy condition.

She placed Nathaniel on the floor and gave him

several of his favorite toys that she'd brought along. With him happily entertained, she got to work.

Jack had just spent the most miserable night of his life. He'd never been good at illness. Edmund had once told him he was the most miserable patient on the face of the earth.

Jack couldn't help it. He hated feeling weak, helpless. He closed his eyes, the sound of activity coming from the kitchen oddly comforting.

His first inclination when Marissa had arrived had been to send her packing. He knew it was guilt that drove her to come here. She should feel guilty.

Hell, that kid of hers had intentionally tripped him up. Jack didn't particularly want to assuage her guilt, nor did he want anything whatsoever to do with her and her child.

But that first impulse to send her packing had changed the moment she'd mentioned breakfast. He hadn't eaten at all when he'd returned home yesterday and this morning he was starving.

No husband, she'd said. So where was the kid's father? Not that he cared. Not that he really wanted to know. He eyed the kitchen doorway. Maybe he should go in there and sort of supervise.

Decision made, he pulled himself up from the sofa and with his crutches hobbled into the kitchen where Marissa was cleaning off a stack of dirty dishes and the kid was sitting on the floor, probably thinking about his next victim.

Marissa turned at the sound of his approach. She flashed him a quick smile. "Afraid I'm after the Coffey silver?"

"Hardly," he replied as he sank into one of the chairs at the table. "If you're looking for silver or china, you've come to the wrong place. I figured I'd better sit in here and watch to make sure Dennis the Menace doesn't set the room on fire while you aren't looking."

He frowned as the kid banged the bottom of an empty pot with a wooden spoon. He hit it several times, then smiled up at Jack, as if awaiting a compliment on his rhythmic skills.

Jack averted his gaze, and within seconds the kid lost interest in the pot and instead played with a set of plastic measuring spoons. Jack focused on the woman busily cleaning up the mess he'd assumed Maria would be cleaning today.

"You don't have to clean up the whole place just to make breakfast," he said.

She turned and smiled once again. "I don't mind. I don't work well in chaos. Besides, I feel partially responsible for you firing your housekeeper this morning."

"Why do you feel responsible?"

Leaning against the counter, she shrugged. "You probably wouldn't have fired her if you hadn't been particularly cranky this morning from your injuries."

He stared at her, surprised at her audacity in

claiming he was cranky. "That's ridiculous," he scoffed. "I'm not more cranky this morning than I ever am. Besides, this is the sixth time I've fired Maria in the last three years. She irritates me on a regular basis. Most people irritate me."

"I still feel partially responsible," she repeated, then turned back around. She poured him a cup of freshly brewed coffee and placed it on the table before him. "Here, maybe coffee will improve your disposition."

"There's nothing wrong with my disposition," he retorted. "I like being cranky."

"Cwanky." The kid beamed up at Jack, rounded blue eyes sparkling with merriment. Sure, the kid was happy. His leg wasn't broken.

Jack sipped his coffee and watched Marissa work. She was clad in a pair of faded cutoffs and a navy short-sleeved blouse. The deep darkness of the blouse accentuated the fairness of her short, curly hair. With the sunlight streaming in through the window and playing on her pale strands, her hair looked like a golden halo.

Yeah, right. An angel of mercy with the kid from hell at her side. Still, he had to admit, the child didn't make an attempt to get into anything, didn't pull open cabinets or climb on the furniture like most toddlers. He seemed perfectly content to sit on the floor and play with the various cooking utensils his mother had given him.

"You live around here?" he asked. Mason Bridge

was a relatively small town. Jack thought he knew, at least by sight, most of the natives.

"No. We're here on vacation. We're from Kansas City." She didn't stop her work as she spoke. "We just arrived yesterday morning."

"Why here? Most vacationers don't even know about Mason Bridge and instead go straight to Miami or one of the other more popular Florida beaches."

"My grandmother visited a friend here once and was charmed by the place. Anyway, we'd just gotten settled on the beach when you had your accident."

"You mean when your kid tried to kill me."

This got her full attention. She turned to face him and her green eyes sparked with a hint of irritation of her own. "His name is Nathaniel. He isn't 'the kid' or 'the monster' or 'Dennis the Menace.' He's Nathaniel Criswell. And it's childish of you to make a two-year-old personally accountable for what was nothing more than an accident."

She looked exceptionally pretty, with her eyes flashing and her cheeks flushed with color. He wondered if her eyes would flash like that when he kissed her. He sat up straighter in his chair, wondering where that particular thought had come from.

He had no intention of kissing Marissa. He had no intention of kissing anyone. He liked his life just fine without complications...and women inevitably became complications.

Still, even though he didn't intend to kiss her, he

couldn't help but admire her backside as she worked. She had long, shapely legs and a rounded behind that wiggled provocatively as she whipped eggs in a mixing bowl, then poured them into a waiting skillet.

"Nathaniel? What kind of a name is that?" he asked. Someplace in the back of his mind, he was aware that he might be picking a fight. But he was comfortable with exasperation. He wasn't comfortable with the stir of desire that had momentarily fluttered through him.

"It's a good name," she replied as she placed a plate in front of him. She smiled, not rising to his obvious baiting. "I named him after Nathaniel Hawthorne." Her smile remained in place, although her eyes glittered with a hint of challenge. "At least it shows a little more imagination than Jack. What kind of name is that?"

He laughed, surprising himself with the rusty-sounding verbalization.

"Now, stop being cantankerous and eat before it gets cold," she exclaimed. She poured him more coffee, then grabbed her son from the floor and put him on the chair next to Jack. "I hope you don't mind if I feed him. He's a social guy. If anyone in the room is eating, he thinks he should eat, too."

Jack shrugged and watched as she took a sash from the sack she'd brought and tied it around the back of the chair, effectively creating a seat belt for the little boy. She handed him half a piece of toast, then poured herself a cup of coffee and joined them at the table.

Jack focused on the food on his plate, awkwardly handling the fork with his left hand. He'd often thought it would be nice to be ambidextrous, but at no time more than now.

He relaxed slightly as he realized she wasn't watching him, but instead was feeding Nathaniel a serving of biscuits and gravy.

For a few minutes the only sound in the room was the little boy's chatter between bites. Jack kept his attention studiously focused away from the boy. However, he did find his gaze going again and again to Marissa.

Her round face was wreathed in a smile as she fed her son. Jack was close enough to her to smell her scent, a fresh fragrance of blooming flowers. Freckles danced across the top of her nose and gave her face a lively quality that was both arresting and girlish.

She was not his type at all. Although he had to admit, it had been so long since he'd been with a woman, he wasn't sure he remembered what his type was.

Still, it intrigued him that his scowls and growls didn't seem to bother her a bit. In fact, she was the only person, other than Edmund, who seemed not only able to take what he gave, but to fling it right back at him.

"So, what do you do back in Kansas City?" He

figured the least he could do was offer a little small talk in exchange for the wonderful breakfast.

"You mean between the care and feeding of the monster child?" Her eyes twinkled with good humor. "I'm a nurse's aide."

A nurse's aide. He shook his head ruefully, remembering how she'd knelt on his hand, then kneed him in the ribs while he'd been lying helpless on the beach. He pitied the patients she worked with.

"I know what you're thinking," she exclaimed, her cheeks flushing a pretty pink. "And I'm very good at what I do." She raised her chin a notch and eyed him defiantly.

"I'll say one thing, you're a terrific cook." He shoved his plate away with a sigh of contentment.

"Thank you. I enjoy cooking. I don't do it very often just for me and Nathaniel."

"So, how long you been divorced?" Jack asked as she wiped Nathaniel's mouth with a napkin.

"I'm not divorced."

"Oh, a widow...I'm sorry."

Her cheeks were becoming a darker shade of pink. "I've never been married."

"Oh, I just assumed..." Jack was embarrassed by his assumption.

"It's a natural assumption." She smiled, that sunny smile that shot a wave of warmth through Jack. "I'm not particularly proud of the fact that I'm not married. But I'm not ashamed, either. I got pregnant. I assumed my boyfriend would be thrilled, and instead, the thought of fatherhood sent him running for the woods.''

There was no trace of bitterness in her voice, but bitterness swept through Jack with a vengeance. There was nothing he hated more than men who ran from their responsibilities as parents...unless it was women who kept men from shouldering those responsibilities and relishing the joys of fatherhood.

He studiously shoved away thoughts of a little boy not much older than Nathaniel...a little boy with dark brown hair and big brown eyes...a little boy Jack hadn't seen for five long years. He couldn't afford to think about him, couldn't stand the pain such thoughts brought with them.

Instead he focused his attention once again on Marissa. Smiling Marissa with the dancing freckles. ''So, I suppose your experience with your boyfriend has made you hate all men. Isn't that the way it usually goes?''

She laughed, a musical chime that awakened desire in him. ''I don't know how it usually goes, but no, I haven't become a man hater.'' She untied the sash that held Nathaniel, kissed his forehead and sat him on the floor.

When she once again gazed at Jack, her eyes were the lush green of spring, the promise of summer warmth and verdant meadows. ''I'm an eternal optimist and I believe in true love and promises kept and vows of forever. All I'm waiting for is to find the right man.''

Jack smiled cynically. He believed in none of those things. Not anymore. "And what are you going to do if you don't find Mr. Right?"

She stood and started clearing off the dishes from the table. "But I will find him. Or he'll find me. And we'll know in an instant of our gazes meeting, our fingers touching, that we're meant for each other." The color of her eyes deepened and a wistful smile lifted the corners of her mouth.

Jack snorted derisively, uncomfortable with how utterly appealing she looked. "You don't really believe that bull, do you?"

"Oh, but I do," she replied. She placed the dishes in the sink, then turned back to face him. "And what does Jack Coffey believe in?"

"Nothing. Absolutely nothing." Jack was aware of the hollowness of his voice and suddenly he was overwhelmed with weariness. He pushed his chair away from the table, grabbed his crutches and stood. "I'm going to lie down. You and Nate can let yourselves out. Thanks for the breakfast."

He started to take a step toward the living room, but was halted by Nathaniel, who launched himself at Jack and wrapped his chubby arms around his leg cast. Marissa had her back to them, filling the sink with soapy water.

Jack looked down at the little boy who momentarily held him captive. "Let go, kid."

Nathaniel grinned, displaying pearly white teeth, but didn't release his hold. Although he wasn't causing Jack any additional pain, Jack was afraid to try to take a step with Nathaniel clinging to him like a burr on a dog.

"Let go," Jack repeated sternly, and scowled down at the little boy. Nathaniel laughed and drew his fuzzy light brows together in a mock imitation of Jack.

Marissa turned from the sink and gasped. "Oh, I'm so sorry." She hurried to them. "Nathaniel, sweetie, let go of Mr. Coffey."

"No." Nathaniel smiled at his mother and pushed his little body tight against the cast. "Daddy," he said, and patted the plaster.

The word, uttered in sweet baby talk, sent a spiraling shaft of pain through Jack. He fought the pain and instead summoned the anger that had always shielded him. "Would you get this kid off me?"

"I'm trying," Marissa said with an embarrassed laugh. She was attempting to peel his arms away from Jack's cast, but Nathaniel was having none of it. He gazed up at Jack with that wide, toothy grin.

"Maybe if you'd try to pick him up," Marissa finally said.

"Up," Nathaniel said, as if agreeing with his mother.

Jack didn't want to pick him up. He didn't want to feel the little boy's snuggly warmth, didn't want to smell that innocent sweetness of childhood. But he also didn't want to spend the rest of his natural life trapped in the kitchen in the clutches of a two-year-old.

With a deep sigh, Jack bent and grabbed the boy, wincing as he tried to use his broken fingers. Nathaniel came willingly into his arms, instantly releasing his hold around Jack's cast and replacing it with a stranglehold around his neck.

Jack tried not to feel, not wanting to experience any of the sensations that came with holding a small child. But it was impossible not to smell the baby scent that wafted from Nathaniel, impossible not to be warmed by the chubby body so close to his heart.

"Take him," Jack demanded of Marissa. "Take him and go."

"But the dishes…" Marissa protested as she worked to take the wailing Nathaniel from him. Marissa stood so close to Jack he could once again smell the sweet scent of her. If he wanted, he could lean forward and kiss her freckles. If he wanted, he could capture her luscious mouth with his. But of course, that was the last thing he wanted.

"Look, you've gone above and beyond the call of duty. I'll manage the rest of the cleanup. Just go." He wanted her gone. He especially wanted the kid gone. Jack had no room in his life for do-gooders with sweet smiles and illusory idealism.

Something about Marissa made him think of deep kisses and warm flesh. Something about Marissa and her child made him recall old hopes, half-remembered dreams.

"You'll be all right?" She raised her voice to be heard over Nathaniel's cries of displeasure.

"I'll be fine," Jack assured her. "I'm going to take a nice long nap and I'll call Maria and hire her back. Trust me. I'll be okay."

She picked up her purse and fished her car keys out of the bottom. She walked to the front door, then turned back to him. "I'm staying at the Mason Bridge Motel, if you need anything. Please don't hesitate to call if there's anything I can do to make things easier for you."

He nodded. The easiest thing she could do for him was to disappear from his life. "Goodbye, Marissa. Have a nice life."

The moment she was gone, Jack was able to breathe easier. "Good riddance," he muttered. He made his way back into the kitchen for a fresh cup of coffee, and that was when he saw it. Nathaniel's diaper bag. The multicolored plastic bag sat on the counter, an indication that she'd be back.

Jack groaned. He didn't know when, but there was no question that Miss Sunshine and her juvenile delinquent would be back.

Chapter Three

Marissa discovered that the diaper bag was missing about an hour later when she went to change Nathaniel's diaper. Drat, she thought as she realized she must have left it at Jack's. She considered driving immediately back to his house, but remembering he'd said he intended to nap, she decided to wait until later.

She took a clean diaper from her suitcase and changed Nathaniel, who'd been cranky ever since they'd left Jack's. The afternoon loomed long before her. She wasn't accustomed to so much free time on her hands.

"So what do you want to do, sweetie?" she asked Nathaniel. Not expecting an answer and not getting one, she moved to the window of her motel room as Nathaniel grabbed some of his toys and sat on the floor.

They could spend a little time on the beach, but the idea of the heat and the sand didn't hold much appeal. Maybe a nap, she thought. Nathaniel was so crabby, a nap would probably do him a lot of good, and her sleep hadn't been exactly restful the night before.

Decision made, she scooped up Nathaniel in her arms and together mother and son stretched out on the bed. She stroked the boy's forehead to stop his wiggling, and within minutes his eyes drifted closed and his breathing became deep and regular.

As he slept, she studied him, finding delight in each and every miniature feature. He was all Criswell, with his round face, fair complexion and light hair. It was as if nature had known his father would reject him and so decided he'd possess none of Bill's physical characteristics.

She rolled over on her back and stared at the ceiling, her thoughts shifting from her son to Jack Coffey. He certainly hadn't been taken with anything about Nathaniel. She'd never seen a man so uncomfortable around a child.

She swallowed a giggle as a mental vision unfolded in her mind…Nathaniel strangling Jack with a hug around the neck, and the resulting stark panic that had swept over Jack's face.

He intrigued her. He was cantankerous, impatient and downright rude, but beneath it all she sensed a vulnerability, an unwillingness to share anything of himself for fear of…fear of what?

She scoffed inwardly. She was obviously allowing her imagination to get the better of her. She knew absolutely nothing about Jack Coffey, and had no desire to get to know him further.

Shaking her head, she tried to clear her mind of his image, but it didn't work. Those blue eyes, so cold when irritated but so warm when amused, were difficult to dismiss. And that smile…it had an edge of wickedness to it that made her body temperature rise in response.

Still, he wasn't anything like the type of man she envisioned as her Mr. Right. She closed her eyes and fought to summon the image that had been her dream man since the day Bill had walked out on her.

She had no real mental image of how her dream man would look, but she knew he'd have a shy smile and gentle eyes. He'd be a soft-spoken man who would have all the ideals she did. They would be two halves of a whole, completely in tune with each other on all issues.

The man she would eventually marry would also adore Nathaniel. He wouldn't call him "the kid" or "the monster" and his features wouldn't radiate panic each time Nathaniel came near.

She had a feeling Jack was rarely in tune with anyone on anything. He'd obviously been born to be a bachelor and she pitied any woman who might try to change his mind on that particular issue.

It was nearly three in the afternoon when Nathaniel awakened Marissa by attempting to wiggle out of her embrace. She caught him just as he was about to plunge headfirst off the end of the bed. "Hey, partner, where are you going?" She tickled his tummy, sending gales of childish laughter into the air.

"You want to go bye-bye?" she asked as she scooped him up and placed him on the floor.

"Bye-bye," Nathaniel agreed, going to the motel-room door and reaching for the doorknob.

Marissa laughed. "Wait a minute, munchkin. I need to clean up a little before we go." Her plan was to go back to Jack's and grab the diaper bag, then she and Nathaniel would take a little drive and find an interesting-looking restaurant for dinner.

It was nearly four by the time she pulled up in front of Jack's house. The beach scene was idyllic. For a moment she stood outside the car, enjoying the peaceful beauty. The waves rolled to the sandy shore, the rhythmic slap audible from where she stood.

Jack must have paid a fortune for the glass-fronted house with its own private beach, she thought. The private investigation business must be a lucrative one.

As she climbed the stairs to the door with Nathaniel in her arms, she hoped Jack had managed to get a nap. He'd looked so tired during breakfast, and there had been moments when dark shadows had stolen the light from his incredibly blue eyes.

In and out, she told herself as she knocked on the door. There was no reason to linger. She'd grab the diaper bag, then be on her way.

"Come in," his voice barked from somewhere in the house.

She opened the door and stepped inside, instantly spying him at the computer workstation. He was clad in a pair of navy cotton shorts and a gray T-shirt and when he turned to look at her, she realized that at some point during the afternoon he'd shaved.

"I figured it was you," he said.

"Yes, it's me," she said inanely, unable to stop staring at his face. Without the cover of the whiskers, he was far more handsome than she'd even imagined. The scruffy facial hair had detracted from his high cheekbones and sensual mouth and had completely hidden a small cleft in his chin.

"What are you staring at?" he asked gruffly.

"Nothing…you…" She flushed. "You shaved."

He raked a hand across his jaw. "Yeah. I took a bath, too. If you want to call it that. I discovered a cast definitely presents a challenge in that particular department."

"You look very nice."

His eyes widened in surprise. "Thanks." Again

his voice was gruff and he turned back around to the computer. "Your bag is in the kitchen," he said.

Nathaniel wiggled in Marissa's arms, wanting to be released. "Down," he demanded.

"No, Nathaniel." Marissa held tighter to the little boy. She went into the kitchen, grabbed the diaper bag, then returned to the living room where Jack was punching computer keys with a single finger.

"Did you call Maria to rehire her?" she asked.

Once again he turned his chair to face her. "I tried to call her, but she wasn't home. Bingo can last for hours, so I figured I'd try to reach her tomorrow."

"Did you manage to nap?"

"Yeah, I slept for a couple of hours."

"Nathaniel and I are on our way to a restaurant for dinner. Would you like to join us?" The invitation sprang from her lips before she was consciously aware of the intent to offer it.

"Can't." His brows pulled together in what had become a familiar frown. "I've got to get this report out in the morning mail and at the rate I'm going, I'll be here all night."

"I offered to help," she reminded him.

"Yeah, you did, didn't you?" He studied her for a moment, his frown deepening. "Does the offer still stand?" The words came slowly, as if pulled from the depths of his stubbornness, and revealing his deep reluctance to admit he needed her help.

"Of course the offer still stands." So much for her plan of a quick stop, she thought.

"Actually, I've got several reports that need to be typed." He didn't look at her.

"Jack, I don't mind helping. Whatever you need done, I'll do."

"I could order in pizza," he suggested.

"Okay," she agreed. She set Nathaniel on the floor and handed him several toys from the diaper bag, then walked over to the workstation. "Just show me what you need done."

"I've got rough drafts of the reports handwritten here." He gestured to a small stack of papers next to him. Marissa leaned forward to look at them.

She was close enough now to smell him, the crisp, clean scent of minty soap mingling with the whisper of a pleasantly male cologne.

He clicked the computer mouse with his left hand. "And here is the report form I use. It's pretty self-explanatory."

She leaned closer to view the monitor, so close she could feel the heat radiating from his body. Again she was struck by his utter, almost overwhelming masculinity.

She tried to concentrate on his explanation of the form, but her attention was captured by the strength in his hand, his sinewy forearm, the bulge of his biceps and the width of his shoulders.

Jack Coffey appeared to be in peak physical condition and Marissa was suddenly reminded of the fifteen extra pounds she'd carried since Nathaniel's birth. Fifteen pounds that absolutely refused to go away.

"Think you can handle it okay?" He turned to look at her and his face was so near, his mouth so close to hers, her breath caught in her chest.

His eyes deepened in hue, becoming dark, drowning depths that beckoned Marissa to fall in. "Yes, I can handle it," she said, her voice seeming to come from a long distance away.

"Good. I've got just one more question."

"What's that?" Marissa fought the need to wet her lips.

"What kind of pizza do you like?"

She straightened, breaking the spell she'd momentarily fallen into. "Pizza?" she echoed. "It doesn't matter. Anything is fine."

Fire burned her cheeks as she moved aside so he could get out of the computer chair. What had she been thinking? That he'd ask her if he could kiss her?

Why on earth would she want Jack Coffey to kiss her? He was nothing more to her than an unlucky victim of an accident, nothing more than a disagreeable man whom fate had momentarily thrown in her path.

"Uh...you'll have to help me keep an eye on Nathaniel," she said. "I can't concentrate on typing and watch him at the same time."

"Can't we just shackle him?" Jack asked dryly.

He held up a hand before she could retort. "Okay, I can tell by the look on your face that's out of the question. I'll keep an eye on him, but if he comes at me wielding anything that remotely resembles a weapon, I'm calling for backup."

Marissa laughed. Under his gruffness, beneath his crusty exterior lurked a delightful sense of humor she could only appreciate. She sobered as she sat on the chair in front of the computer.

She had a feeling it would be in her best interest to type the reports quickly and put as much distance as possible between her and Jack.

Okay, she could admit to herself that physically he was quite appealing. And she'd go further and admit that she apparently was vulnerable to the flutter of sexual tension he created in her. But he certainly wasn't the kind of man she'd want in her life for anything long-term.

Her relationship with Bill had been stupid. Falling into anything remotely resembling a relationship with Jack would be sheer insanity.

She smiled inwardly, amused that a single moment of locked gazes between them could invoke such serious contemplation.

She'd type his reports, share a pizza, then be done with him and get back to her vacation. With this thought in mind, she placed her hands on the keyboard and began to type.

Jack leaned back on the sofa and stretched his leg out on the coffee table, a mean feat as he maneuvered around the accumulated trash that littered the surface.

He hadn't meant to ask Marissa to stay and help him out, but after an hour of struggling to type, he'd been desperate.

He frowned as Nathaniel stood and approached him, a miniature plastic truck in his chubby little hand. If it had been a metal truck, Jack would have been worried.

"Twuck." Nathaniel held the vehicle out to Jack.

"Yeah," Jack replied absently, his gaze going to the woman at the computer.

There had been a brief moment when they'd been so close together that all he'd been able to think about was kissing her. It had been a momentary lapse into derangement, and thankfully he hadn't followed through on the impulse.

Still, what that impulse had prompted him to think about was the monklike way he'd been living for the past several years.

What he needed was to find a woman who believed in the same things he did: no commitments, no emotional entanglements, just good old-fashioned lust.

He knew with certainty that Marissa Criswell would not understand those particular rules. She would not only expect, she would demand emotional involvement. Besides, she was here only for the next couple of weeks, then she'd return to her life in Kansas City and her hopes of finding Mr. Right.

If Jack was lucky, he might be able to manipulate her guilt over his accident to get a couple more home-cooked meals out of her before she left the area.

Thinking of meals, he grabbed the phone and punched in the number for his favorite pizza place. It took him only a minute to order a supreme thick-crust pie. He hung up, then jumped in surprise as Nathaniel climbed up on the sofa next to him.

"Twuck," Nathaniel repeated, and held out the truck to Jack. His appealing blue eyes held Jack's gaze without flinching, in complete concentration as only a small child could do.

With a feeling of resignation, fighting against distant memories that brought with them both pleasure and pain, Jack took the truck.

Nathaniel beamed his approval, then pointed to his mother. "Mommy."

"Yeah, right. That's your mommy," Jack agreed. It had been five years since Jack had been around a child Nathaniel's age.

For the past five years Jack had consciously made decisions that would keep him isolated from children. He didn't eat in family restaurants, he didn't go to the zoo or to amusement parks. But there was no way to avoid this child who seemed insistent to make a connection with him.

"Light." Nathaniel pointed to the light overhead. Jack nodded, wondering if they were going to go through Nathaniel's entire repertoire of speaking words and pointing to the appropriate objects.

Nathaniel got to his feet next to Jack, leaning into the sofa cushion at the back and against Jack's side. "Daddy," he said. Without warning, he grabbed the end of Jack's nose. His tiny fingernails felt like crab pincers and Jack yelped in protest.

"Let go," he exclaimed.

"Daddy!" Nathaniel's fingers didn't release their hold.

Marissa swung around to see what was going on and gasped. She jumped up and hurried to the sofa. "Nathaniel, let go!" she demanded.

Nathaniel offered her an angelic smile. "Daddy," he repeated.

"No, he's not your daddy," Marissa replied. She leaned across Jack to grab her son's wrist.

Tingles of electricity soared through Jack as her breasts made intimate contact with his chest. He could almost make himself believe that being noseless was worth this single moment of pleasure.

All too quickly, she managed to disengage Nathaniel from his nose and with a stern expression set the boy on the floor. "Not nice," she said to him, then turned back to Jack.

"Are you all right?" Once again she leaned over him to inspect the damage. She was so close to him he could see the gold flecks that accentuated the green tint of her eyes. Her mouth was slightly parted as if awaiting a lover's kiss, and he could feel the warmth of her breath on his face.

Her fingers were soft as they touched either side of his nose, and suddenly she was too damned close, too damned attractive.

"I'm fine," he said, waving her away irritably. Her cheeks flushed pink as she stepped away. "Unless you think I need a rabies shot," he added.

"I don't think that will be necessary," she said, unable to hide the amusement that sparkled in her eyes and lifted the corners of her mouth.

"You'd better find that Mr. Right of yours pretty quickly. That boy has a daddy fixation."

"Daddy," Nathaniel said, and pointed to Jack.

"He must have picked this up at day care," she said, a tiny wrinkle of concern appearing in her forehead. "I didn't even know he knew what a daddy was."

Before he could say anything further on the subject, there was a knock on the door. "That should be the pizza," he said. He grabbed his wallet from the coffee table and pulled out a twenty-dollar bill. "Do you mind?" He held out the money and gestured toward the door.

"Of course not." She took the bill and went to the door. She returned with the pizza and paused in the doorway between the living room and kitchen. "Where do you want to eat? In here or in the kitchen?"

"Why don't we eat on my deck," he suggested.

He could still feel the heat from her breasts against his chest, smell her fragrance in the air. The interior of the house suddenly felt too warm, too close, too small. He needed to be outside, in the fresh air.

"A deck?" She looked worriedly toward Nathaniel. "You wouldn't be luring us out onto a deck for any particular reason, would you?"

He laughed. "I promise you, I won't toss the kid overboard. Besides, the deck is completely closed in, so he can't even accidentally fall."

"Okay. Sounds good," she agreed.

"Why don't you bring Nate and then come back for the pizza," he suggested. He started down the hallway. "Come on, the deck is off one of the bedrooms."

"How many bedrooms do you have?" she asked as she followed him with Nate in her arms.

"Three," he replied. He went past one closed door, then another, then turned into his own bedroom. It was a large room with sliding glass doors that led out to an oversize deck overlooking the beach.

He often sat out there in the evenings, watching darkness steal away the blue sky, fighting sleep that all too often was filled with tormenting dreams.

Although his bed was not made, the room was relatively clean. Sleep was the only activity that took place here. He opened the sliding glass door and gestured her outside.

"Oh, this is beautiful," she exclaimed, her eyes

lighting with pleasure as she took in the ocean scene before her. Jack felt a momentary pride. "You have such a beautiful home, and this view is magnificent."

"Don't get scenery like this in Kansas City, do you?"

She smiled and put Nathaniel down. "Unfortunately not. Why don't you get comfortable and I'll go get the pizza and something to drink."

"Beer for me," he replied. "And if you don't want a beer there should be some soda in the fridge." He eased down into one of the chairs.

It had definitely been a good idea to come outside to eat. He wouldn't be able to smell Marissa's perfume out here. The light breeze was rife with the scents of salt water and seaweed. Hopefully the fresh air and warm sunshine would banish any lingering rush of desire he'd experienced for Marissa.

Nathaniel stood and toddled over to Jack. "Nose," he said, and touched the end of his own nose.

"Yeah, kid, you tried to break mine."

"Ear." Nathaniel grabbed his ear.

"What are you doing? Trying to show me how smart you are?" Before Jack could block it, an image unfolded in his mind...the vision of another little boy, a boy with dark hair and brown eyes.

Bobby. His son. Bobby had enjoyed playing the same game Nathaniel was playing. He'd point to his ears, his eyes, his nose, then to his tummy.

"Tummy," he'd say, and pull up his shirt to expose the rounded potbelly. That was Jack's cue to tickle Bobby and he'd tickle that sweet little belly until Bobby was giggling with delight.

Emotion rose inside Jack, filling his throat. He stared out at the ocean, the view shimmering with the burden of thick, choking sentiment.

He tensed as Nathaniel moved closer to him, leaning his sturdy body against Jack's leg. The little boy laid his head against Jack's side and a chubby hand patted Jack's cast.

Jack nearly came undone. He wanted to shove Nate away to escape the emotions that exploded inside him. He wanted to grab him up and hug him, revel in the sweet scent of babyhood that still clung to him, lose himself in the emotions that exploded inside him.

He moved a hand across the top of Nate's head, feeling the silky-soft baby hair. He closed his eyes, fighting the waves of pain that assaulted him.

Bobby...Bobby, where are you? The question called from deep within his soul.

"Here we are."

Marissa's voice pulled Jack back from the abyss of his grief. His eyes snapped open and he dropped the hand that had been caressing Nate's head.

"Just in time," he said, his voice gravelly and deeper than usual.

She carried the pizza box topped with two bottles of beer, two glasses and a tippy cup filled with what appeared to be grape juice. "Is he hurting your leg?" she asked as she set the tray on the table.

"Not yet, but I don't take anything for granted where he's concerned." He breathed a sigh of relief as she scooped up Nate in her arms, then deposited him on his bottom on the floor of the deck. She opened the box of pizza, tore off the crust from a piece and handed it to him.

With Nate happily occupied, she sat down at the table next to Jack and opened his beer for him. "Bottle or glass?" she asked.

He eyed her dryly. "Do you really think I'm a glass kind of guy?" She handed him the bottle.

For the next few minutes they didn't speak, but rather concerned themselves with devouring the pizza. The only sounds were the distant rhythmic splash of waves meeting shore and an occasional cry from a bird overhead.

Jack felt himself relaxing inch by inch, gaining distance from the emotional past he'd momentarily fallen into.

The pizza was warm, the beer cold and at the moment nothing on his body ached or hurt.

"Have you lived here long?" Marissa asked as she finished her second piece of pizza, breaking the silence that had fallen between them.

"My parents bought the place when I was nine, and we spent every summer here. It always felt like home more than any other place we lived. I moved here permanently almost eight years ago."

"Have you always been a private investigator?" she asked.

"No. I was a cop for five years, then five years ago I quit the force and hung out my shingle as a private eye."

She eyed him curiously. "What made you decide to do that?"

He frowned and stared out at the rolling waves in the distance. "I just felt like it." His tone was more harsh than he'd intended. But he didn't apologize. There were some things that, as far as he was concerned, were off-limits. And his past was one of them.

"I guess I'd better get back to those reports," she said as she stood. "I apologize for intruding on your privacy."

Jack frowned. Her apology made him feel small and fractious. "No, I apologize. I'm just not accustomed to sharing small talk with a woman. Sharing little pieces often leads to familiarity, and familiarity often leads to complications that don't interest me."

Marissa stared at him for a long moment, then threw back her head and laughed. "I don't believe it," she exclaimed. "You're actually afraid that somehow I'll fall for you." She laughed again, an incredulous edge to her laughter.

"I don't see what's so damned funny," Jack answered indignantly.

She stepped close to him and placed a hand on his arm. "Trust me, Jack. You have nothing to worry about. You are nothing like the man I intend to fall in love with. At this point, I'm not even sure I like you very much.'' Still laughing, she picked up Nathaniel and left the deck.

Jack stared after her, wondering why it irritated him that a woman he hadn't even known two days ago was so certain she could never, ever fall for him.

Chapter Four

Marissa did her best to concentrate on typing the reports, but her gaze kept shifting from the reports to Jack, who sat on the sofa staring into space.

Evening had fallen, and when he'd come in from the deck he'd turned on the interior lights to ward off the approaching darkness. Despite the illumination, the shadows of evening seemed to have taken up residence on Jack's features.

She wondered if he were in pain, and for the hundredth time guilt soared through her. She couldn't believe how fast her son had managed to take out a grown man.

The guilty party had cooperated by falling sound asleep in the middle of the living-room floor. As Nathaniel slept, he snored faintly, the sound indicating his sleep was peaceful and deep.

It was hard for Marissa to believe how easily her son had taken to Jack. Nathaniel didn't seem to be a bit bothered by Jack's gruff voice or deep scowls.

Marissa frowned and focused once again on the last report she was trying to finish. She read Jack's notes, then looked at him. "You really followed this woman, Beth Daniels, everywhere for four days?"

Jack returned her gaze. "Everywhere. I sat outside the beauty shop while she got her hair done, followed her to the cleaners. I watched her eat lunch with her best friend from high school and sat behind her in the movie theater where she ate half a container of popcorn and a whole box of Milk Duds."

"And she never suspected she was being followed?"

Jack grinned, the gesture making pinpoints of light dance in his eyes. "I told you I was good."

"I would know if somebody was following me," Marissa exclaimed.

He leaned forward. "Not if it were me," Jack argued, a wicked gleam in his blue eyes. "I told you, I'm good." He leaned back once again. "In that particular case, Beth Daniels's husband hired me to find out if she was cheating on him."

Marissa picked up the photos that were to accompany the report. One showed an attractive blond woman standing at a motel-room door. The next showed the door being opened by a tall, dark-haired man, and the third caught the woman slipping through the door. "I guess she was."

"Yeah," Jack agreed. "The third night of surveillance while her husband was at a business dinner, Mrs. Daniels apparently had an intimate little dinner of her own."

Marissa set the photographs down, her frown deepening. "Why didn't Mr. Daniels just ask his wife what was going on in her life?"

Jack stared at Marissa in obvious disbelief. "Because women lie."

There was a vehemence in his voice that stunned Marissa. "Not all women lie," she protested. "This just seems rather..."

"Sleazy?" Jack's eyebrows rose and a mocking smile curved his lips. "I'm a sleazy kind of guy who does a sleazy kind of job."

Marissa flushed. "That wasn't what I was going to say. I was going to say that this all seems rather sad, that it takes a third party to find out the truth between two people who are married and supposed to love each other."

The mocking smile remained on Jack's lips. "In my line of work and in my vast experience, I've realized that love is just a fantasy people pretend to feel to fill unhealthy emotional needs."

"Surely you don't really believe that," she protested. There was something in the depths of his blue eyes that had nothing to do with mockery, but rather spoke of betrayal and pain. He broke eye contact and looked away, as if afraid of what she might see there.

"I do believe that," he replied. He looked at her once again, and whatever vulnerability she'd thought she'd seen in his eyes was gone. "Love is a fantasy, a concept created by poets and expanded on by the entertainment industry. The only marriages that last are built on mutual financial interests and common goals and interests."

Marissa stared at him in disbelief and sighed, his cynicism evoking a strange sadness inside her. What would it be like to live without the hope of finding true love? It certainly had to be a cold, barren place in which to exist.

"You are some piece of work, Jack Coffey. If I was to hazard a guess, I'd say somebody hurt you really badly."

He laughed. "And if I had to hazard a guess, I'd say you were seriously stunted in the reality department. You of all people should know love isn't real. You bought into the concept of true love forever more and look where it's gotten you. You're now a single parent because you believed in the foolishness of love."

"That's not true," Marissa exclaimed. "I'm a single parent because I made the mistake of falling in love with the wrong man, not because I believed in love. I won't make the same mistake again."

"That's right." His voice was heavy with sarcasm. "Next time you'll know Mr. Right as soon as you meet him."

"That's right," she agreed, ignoring his derision.

"And we'll spend the rest of our lives deeply in love and happy." The conviction of her intense belief rang in her voice.

"Have you always been delusional?"

She laughed, finding the entire debate stimulating in a strange sort of way. "One of us is definitely delusional, but if I were you, I wouldn't be so quick to point a finger at me."

He grinned at her, a genuine smile that deepened the cleft in his chin and caused a starburst of heat to explode in the pit of her stomach. "I'm not delusional, Marissa. I'm just a nonbeliever when it comes to fairy tales like love."

Marissa returned his grin. "Then I hope someday the love bug takes a big bite out of you and changes your mind."

Again she thought she saw a whisper of vulnerability, a shadow of pain in Jack's eyes. But it was there only an instant, then gone, replaced by the hard sheen of cynicism. "Not in this lifetime." Anything else he intended to say was halted by the ringing of the telephone.

Jack grabbed the receiver of the phone on the nearby end table while Marissa focused once again on the report on the computer screen.

"What?"

She shook her head ruefully at Jack's surly greeting to whomever was on the other end of the line. Jack Coffey was definitely some piece of work.

"When?"

She felt Jack's sudden tension as he sat up straighter against the sofa cushions. She finished the last report, but hesitated hitting the Print icon, sensing that his conversation was important.

"I'll see what I can do. Thanks for the heads-up." He slammed down the phone, then slapped the cast on his leg. "Damn."

"What's wrong?" Marissa asked.

"What's wrong?" Jack struggled to his feet. "What's wrong is that a man I've been trying to find for the past year is supposed to show up someplace tomorrow morning and I have a cast on my leg that makes driving a car and conducting a stakeout impossible."

"I could drive you," she offered.

He glared at her as if she'd lost what little sense he'd thought she possessed. "You can drive me," he repeated flatly. "And what do you know about conducting a stakeout."

She shrugged. "Only what I've seen in movies. You buy a bunch of junk food, sit in a car across from the place you're watching, and wait."

A reluctant grin curved Jack's lips. "That's about right." The grin disappeared and a thoughtful crease lined his forehead. "It's not dangerous at all," he said more to himself than to her. "But it could be a very long, boring day."

"Imagine the fun of being able to tell everyone back home that I went on a real stakeout on my vacation."

Marissa wasn't sure why she wanted to do this. Perhaps because she still felt responsible for Jack's injuries. Or maybe it was because something in the darkness of his eyes challenged her to bring him light.

"Okay." Jack relented. "If this wasn't so important and if I hadn't waited so long to find this guy, I wouldn't dream of taking you up on your offer."

"But since I offered—" she flashed him a quick smile "—and you have no other alternative, you'll take my offer."

"Right." His gaze left hers and shot to Nathaniel. "I don't suppose you'd consider leaving him in your motel room for the duration of the stakeout?"

"Not a chance," she said, wondering when she'd stopped being offended by his derogatory remarks about her son. Maybe it had been the moment she'd walked out on the deck and had seen Jack caressing Nathaniel's head.

"And the only restraint I'll agree to is his car seat," she added before he could suggest some other form of bondage for the little guy.

"And he can't get out of his car seat without help?"

Marissa laughed. "No. I promise, Jack. I'll keep you safe from Nathaniel." She clicked the Print command on the computer screen and stood. "That's the last of your reports."

"Thanks, I appreciate the help."

"What time do you want me here in the morning for the stakeout?" she asked.

"Around six."

She winced. "Then I'd better get right back to the motel and get some sleep." She stooped to pick up the sleeping child. Nathaniel stirred only long enough to wrap his arms around her neck, then fell back sound asleep.

Jack grabbed the diaper bag and Marissa's purse and with them hanging from the handles of his crutches walked her to the front door. He handed her the items. "You sure you're up for this?"

"Absolutely," she replied without hesitation.

"Then I guess I'll see you in the morning," he said.

She nodded. "Bright and early." She turned to leave.

"Marissa?" She turned back to him, paused at the top of the narrow staircase. "Thanks again for all your help." He smiled and once again she felt an explosion of fire in her stomach.

"You're welcome," she replied, then turned and headed down the stairs toward her car. Her knees felt weak as she took the steps slowly. That smile of his, void of cynicism, genuine and full, had the power to muddle her senses and shoot electricity through her veins.

She buckled Nathaniel into his car seat, then slid behind the steering wheel. Looking up at the house, she could see Jack standing in the doorway, and the heat that had momentarily suffused her intensified.

Even with crutches and the cast on his leg, he looked strong and sexy. The memory of his scent, a wild, slightly spicy fragrance, returned to her and for a moment she wondered what it would be like to be held in his arms, stroked with his hands, kissed with his lips.

"What's wrong with me?" she muttered as she started the engine. When Jack smiled so genuinely, causing his eyes to light like blue stars and the cleft in his chin to deepen provocatively, it did something to Marissa.

She wondered what Jack would be like with a smile on his face all the time. What would he be like with hope filling his heart? The possibility stole her breath away.

As she drove away from the house, she thought of the morning to come. Who knew how long she'd be cooped up in the car with Jack?

She'd promised she'd keep Jack safe from Nathaniel, but who was going to keep her safe from Jack Coffey?

Jack sat on his deck, watching the sun peek over the edge of the horizon, sending vibrant pinks and golds across the lingering night sky, the colors reflected on the surface of the water.

Marissa should be pulling up any time, and he had spent the night regretting accepting her offer to drive him and spend whatever time it took on the stakeout.

If it wasn't for the fact that Jack had been after Samuel Jacobson for the past year and now might possibly be in a position to get the scum arrested, he would never have considered Marissa's offer.

He sighed and raked a hand through his hair. He'd slept relatively well last night, but had been visited with dreams. Disturbing dreams of Marissa.

In those dreams he'd been kissing her sweet lips and running his hands through her blond halo of silky curls. Her eyes had been the inviting green of deep summer, promising a heady heat and over-whelming pleasure.

And in his dream he'd taken her heat, fallen into the pleasure of her kiss, her caresses. He'd awak-ened horrified, not so much by the dream itself, but rather by the burst of joy that had accompanied the dream. A joy he hadn't experienced for a long time, a joy he'd believed he would never feel again.

When the last of the dream images had left his mind, he'd scoffed at his own emotions. Marissa, with all her talk of Mr. Right and love forevermore, had apparently seeped into his subconscious mind. But in his conscious mind he knew better than to fall for the fantasy.

"Been there, done that," he muttered to the new morning. And he'd never be fool enough to fall for the fantasy again.

It had taken him five years to recover when his

life had fallen apart. He wasn't about to allow one sexy blonde with dewy eyes and crazy dreams to disrupt the tentative peace he'd finally managed to find for himself.

What he couldn't figure out was how a woman he'd known less than three days had managed to invade his dreams. It was ridiculous.

He looked at his watch and stood. It was exactly six, and he had a feeling Marissa would be prompt. He walked through his bedroom and to the front door. He gazed out the door just in time to see her rental car pulling up out front.

He hadn't maneuvered the stairs since the day she'd brought him home from the hospital. Going up somehow seemed easier than going down. Falling upstairs held less chance for damage than falling down. He'd left one crutch in his bedroom, figuring by now he needed only one. He gripped the crutch tightly and started down.

He'd reached the third stair when Marissa magically appeared before him. "Let me help you," she said. Before he could protest, she took the crutch from him and instead placed herself beneath his arm. "Now lean on me," she demanded.

She fit perfectly beneath his shoulder, her blond curls tickling the side of his neck. The smell of her, a clean, fresh scent with a whisper of floral perfume, enveloped him, and the warmth of her body against his sparked flames in the pit of his stomach.

"Are you doing all right?" she asked when they were halfway down the staircase.

He grimaced. "As well as can be expected, considering what you and your kid have put me through." His tone was sharper, more gruff than he'd intended.

He saw a flash of answering fire in her eyes, but she said nothing. He almost wished she would get angry with him, exchange barbs of ire with him so he could get rid of some of the energy that coursed through him at the moment.

As he slid into the passenger seat while Marissa stowed his crutch in the trunk, he felt mean-spirited and small. Nathaniel greeted him from his car seat in the back. "Daddy," he said, and laughed.

"Wrong, kid. Jerk is more like it," Jack mumbled in reply.

Marissa slid behind the steering wheel, studiously refusing to look at him. She started the engine.

"Go on. Say it."

She turned and looked at him curiously. "Say what?"

"Tell me I'm a jerk."

"Okay. Jack, you're a jerk." Her eyes glistened with a touch of good humor. "Now you feel better?"

"Yeah, I do." He adjusted the seat to give him more leg room for his cast. "Don't you ever hold a grudge?"

"Not really. I try not to expend energy on negative emotions.'' She put the car into gear and drove away from Jack's house. ''Besides,'' she said, shooting him a teasing side-glance, ''if I held a grudge against you every time you were cranky or said something ugly, I'd be completely exhausted.''

''Still, I was out of line and I apologize.'' He tunneled a hand through his hair. ''I just hate feeling so...so...''

''Helpless?''

''Yeah.'' Surely it was the feeling of helplessness that had attacked him on the stairs. It had absolutely nothing to do with any desire he might feel for the Pollyanna sitting next to him.

''When you get to the intersection up ahead, take a left,'' he said.

As she concentrated on driving, he focused on looking at her. The early-morning light enhanced the gold of her hair and gave her skin a healthy glow. He couldn't discern any makeup except for a slight darkening of her long lashes and a sheen to her lips.

She wore a pair of worn cutoffs and a green T-shirt that looked as if it had been through the wash cycle many times. ''How long did you say you were here on vacation?'' he asked.

''Three glorious weeks.'' She flashed him a quick smile. ''My grandmother gifted me with the vacation. Otherwise I'd have never been able to afford it on my own.''

Now it all made more sense. He hadn't figured her for the normal moneyed vacationer. A gift of what had probably been a much-needed vacation, and he was taking up her time making her feel guilty for an accident that really wasn't anyone's fault.

"I promise you after today, I won't take up another minute of your vacation time," he said.

She flashed him a quicksilver smile. "I don't mind. I have a feeling it wouldn't have taken me long to grow bored of the beach. And with Nathaniel, options for other forms of entertainment are rather limited."

"Go right up here," Jack said, pointing to the nearby intersection.

He gazed at her once again, finding it easy to look at her. "I'll bet you're a good nurse's aide."

"What makes you say that?"

"I don't know. It's easy to imagine you flitting from patient to patient, dispensing cheer and optimism along with pills and shots."

She laughed. "I don't flit, but I like to think I'm good at what I do, and part of my job is tending patients' emotional needs as well as their medical needs."

Jack had a few needs he wouldn't mind her attending to. He pointed for her to take the next right turn, not wanting his mind to dwell on the fact that he found her more attractive than any woman he'd met in the past five years.

"So, who are we going to stake out?" she asked.

Jack shifted position in an attempt to make himself more comfortable. "His name is Samuel Jacobson, and we're going to a house he owns but hasn't lived in the past six months. That phone call last night was from an informant of sorts who said Samuel is going to be at the house sometime today. All I intend to do is see if he shows up, then call a friend of mine on the police force and he'll come and make an arrest." He pulled a cell phone from his pocket to show her.

"An arrest? So this man is a criminal?" She cast him a worried glance.

"Strictly white-collar stuff. I told you yesterday, this is not a dangerous assignment." He grinned at her. "I might be a jerk, but I'm not totally without a conscience. I would never have agreed to you and Nate being with me if I thought there was even a hint of danger."

She flashed him a grateful smile and he wondered if she'd taste as sweet as she looked. Would her lips be warm and soft? Would they open eagerly beneath his? Would she wind her arms around his neck, press her body intimately against his? He shoved these disturbing thoughts aside.

She was here on vacation and in less than three weeks would return to her life back in Kansas City. She'd probably eventually marry a doctor and live her happily-ever-after.

Besides, all Jack wanted from her was a night. One single night of unemotional lust, one solitary night of uncomplicated indulgence of physical pleasure.

Nathaniel let out a loud cry from the backseat, as if he'd been privy to Jack's thoughts and was voicing his protest.

"He's probably hungry," Marissa said. She pointed to the plastic grocery bag between her and Jack. "There's a couple of bananas in there. Would you mind peeling one and giving it to him?"

"Nana," Nathaniel said, and nodded his head.

Jack rummaged in the bag, finding not only bananas, but also hard candy, licorice, a bag of chips, a container of mints and several sausage sticks. "Did you pick this all up on the way to my place?" he asked as he grabbed one of the bananas and peeled it.

She nodded. "A stakeout just isn't a stakeout without a bunch of junk food."

Jack turned and handed Nathaniel the peeled banana. "Daddy." Nathaniel grinned at him and took a bite of the fruit.

"Not in this lifetime, kid," Jack replied. He turned back around to face the front. "Okay…slow down. We're approaching the house."

In the past six months Jack had been in this quiet, upper middle class neighborhood dozens of times, always hoping to find some sign of life in the Jacobson house.

"It's the gray house just ahead. Pull to the curb there, next to that large tree," he instructed. Although they were two houses away from the Jacobson place, this vantage point gave them a perfect view of the two-story house and the driveway. "You can go ahead and cut the engine," he said.

She did, then moved her seat back, allowing her more leg room. She had great legs…long, with tanned skin that looked soft as silk. His fingers itched as he imagined stroking that skin.

Irritation whipped through him. What the hell was wrong with him? Why was this particular woman getting under his skin so effectively?

She'd already told him he wasn't her type, that he certainly wasn't Mr. Right material. And he certainly didn't believe in finding a Mrs. Right for himself.

So why did he have the sudden desire to convince her that he could at least be her Mr. Right For One Night?

Chapter Five

Marissa hadn't considered how close the quarters would be in a car, but as the minutes—hours—passed, she found herself acutely conscious of Jack.

His scent filled the confines of the car, a clean, masculine fragrance that was pleasant. As usual, his hair was in charming disarray, giving him a virile, outdoorsy look that Marissa couldn't help but find attractive.

He was clad in a pair of jogging shorts and gray T-shirt that exposed the tanned muscles of his arms. The cast that encased his leg did nothing to detract from the utter strength and masculinity he emitted.

Restless energy radiated from him, making her feel edgy and tense.

She wondered if Nathaniel sensed the energy, as

well. He was fussier than usual. He rubbed his eyes, threw his banana on the floor and emitted the sounds of a little boy who desperately needed a nap.

"What's wrong with him?" Jack asked as Marissa twisted in her seat for the third time in as many minutes to try to still the unhappy child.

Marissa looked at her watch. "This is about the time he usually takes a morning nap. For some reason, he's fighting it." She gave Nathaniel one of his favorite toys, but he threw it on the floor and continued to whine.

"Maybe if I hold him for a little while," she said, not wanting the little boy's crying to get on Jack's nerves. She twisted around in her seat and with a huge effort managed to unbuckle Nathaniel and pull him over into the front seat and onto her lap.

She pressed Nathaniel's head down against her chest and patted his back, hoping to get him to fall asleep. But he stiffened against her, fighting any and all attempts she made to calm him.

"Hand him to me."

Marissa stared at Jack. "You don't intend to throw him out the window, do you?" she asked dubiously.

He grinned at her, that sexy smile that for some reason seemed to raise her internal temperature. "I promise if the urge to throw him out the window strikes me, I'll let you know before I follow through on it. Just give him to me for a few minutes."

Nathaniel went willingly to Jack and sat in his lap.

"Okay, Nate. What's going on?" Jack asked.

Nathaniel stopped whining and stared at Jack, his blue eyes round as saucers.

"Don't you know real men don't cry?" Jack said.

"I don't believe that," Marissa said. "Real men express their emotions, even if it makes them cry, and that's what I intend to teach Nathaniel."

"Ah." Jack looked from Marissa back to Nathaniel. "Now I see why you're upset. Your mama intends to make you a sissy."

Marissa laughed and Nathaniel grinned, as if he understood the entire conversation and found it vastly amusing.

"You're a mess, Jack Coffey," Marissa exclaimed.

"Hear that, Nate? Your mom is maligning me. What are you gonna do about it?"

Nathaniel stared at Jack for another long moment, then leaned his head against Jack's chest and closed his eyes. Within seconds he was sound asleep.

"Typical male," Marissa said. "When the going gets rough, he goes to sleep."

Jack said nothing, but lightly patted Nathaniel's back. The little boy snuggled closer.

Marissa frowned and stared out the window at the house they were watching. Jack Coffey confused her. He professed to hate children, yet seemed to have a natural way with Nathaniel.

Seeing her son snuggled against Jack's broad chest touched her, made a strange yearning stir deep inside her. The Mr. Right of her dreams would be good with Nathaniel. He would love her son as he loved her. But of course her Mr. Right was nothing like Jack.

"So, what did this Samuel Jacobson do? Take a cruise on company funds? Pad his expense account?" she asked, trying to focus on something other than her son in Jack's strong arms.

Jack stared out the window at the house, not answering for a long moment. "He's a deadbeat dad," he finally said with a frown.

Marissa turned and looked at him in surprise. "A deadbeat dad?"

"He's got a place in Florida, a house in the Cayman Islands. He owns a Mercedes and a boat big enough to house a family of four. And he's got an ex-wife who's living with their two children in a cramped apartment. She's financially struggling and he refuses to pay child support. He's got several judgments and bench warrants out on him."

"So the ex-wife hired you to find him?"

Again Jack hesitated before answering. "No, she doesn't have the kind of money it takes to trail an errant ex-husband. I do some volunteer work for an organization that helps mothers obtain their child support."

Marissa eyed him thoughtfully. The man was a bundle of contradictions and surprises. He was a man who professed to hate children, yet volunteered his valuable time and skills on their behalf.

What other surprises might he offer? One thing was certain, there was more to Jack Coffey than he pretended.

"How did you know he might be here today?" she asked curiously.

"Over the last couple of months, I've made friends with his neighbors." Jack pointed toward the house next to Samuel Jacobson's. "Samuel always calls them to let them know when he's going to be in town for a day or two. He likes the house aired out and asks them to open a couple of windows. Anyway, that's the call I got last night, from the neighbor telling me he'd spoken to Samuel."

Marissa nodded. "You want me to move him to the backseat?" she asked, gesturing to her sleeping child.

"Nah, he's all right. As long as he doesn't elbow me and break a rib or stretch and poke out my eye."

"I think you're safe." Marissa reached into the sack of goodies and pulled out a bag of red licorice. She opened the package and offered him a piece, but he shook his head.

"So, what made you decide to volunteer for this particular organization?" she asked, then took a bite of the licorice stick.

"I don't know. Seemed like a worthy cause."

She smiled teasingly. "I have to admit, I'm surprised. You seem more the type to work for a group like Grouches Have Rights, Too."

He winced in mock pain. "I deserve that. I haven't exactly put my best foot forward with you, have I?"

"It's difficult to put your best foot forward when that foot is broken."

Jack grinned and started to say something in return, but stopped as a car pulled into the driveway of the house they'd been watching.

A short, overweight, balding man got out of the car and unlocked the front door, then disappeared inside.

"Is that him?" Marissa asked eagerly.

"That's him." Jack pulled his cell phone from his pocket and punched in several numbers. "Come and get him," he said to whoever answered his call.

He hung up, then smiled at Marissa. "Now we just wait and watch and hope my buddy gets here before old Samuel decides to take off again."

Within minutes a police car pulled up in front and two burly officers got out of the vehicle and approached the house. They disappeared inside and Marissa found herself holding her breath.

"Yes," Jack hissed as the officers stepped out of the house, Samuel Jacobson in handcuffs. He slapped his knee and grinned at Marissa, a full-bodied smile of triumph. "We finally got him!"

Joy swept through Marissa. "What happens now?" she asked.

"Samuel Jacobson will face an irate judge, and we go home and I fix you a celebratory lunch."

"Sounds good to me. Let me just get him back in his car seat." Marissa reached over and grabbed Nathaniel, who still slept soundly.

He was too heavy for her to attempt to lift over the seat, so she got out of the car, settled him in the back, then got back behind the wheel.

"What's for lunch?" she asked as she started the engine.

"You like Chinese?"

"Love it," she replied.

"Good, I'll order in from my favorite take-out place." She felt his gaze lingering on her. "Marissa...thanks for everything you've done to help me out."

"You're welcome," she replied, trying to ignore the burst of heat that warmed the pit of her stomach. Jack Coffey cranky was one thing. Jack Coffey gracious was downright dangerous.

When they got back to Jack's house, Nathaniel was still sleeping. Marissa carried him into the living room and placed him on the floor.

"What do you want me to order for you?" Jack asked from the kitchen.

"Anything. Surprise me," she replied as she covered Nathaniel with a light blanket.

"If you want to wash up, help yourself," Jack said. "I'll just call in the order."

Marissa started down the hallway to find the bathroom. She knew the room at the end of the hallway was Jack's bedroom, but she wasn't sure which of the other three closed doors was the bathroom.

She opened the first door on her right and froze in the doorway, shock sweeping through her. It wasn't the bathroom—rather, it was a child's room.

A wallpaper border of dancing bears lined the ceiling and a wooden crib with a matching blanket stood against one wall. A toddler bed was along the other wall, the top of it covered with a variety of items.

Someplace in the back of her mind she knew she should step back, close the door, but intense curiosity drew her into the room as she tried to make sense of what she was looking at.

Teddy bears, a toy truck, a miniature fire engine, a baseball glove, clothes in a variety of sizes, everything still in its original box or package. Why was it in here? Who was it for?

Why did Jack, a man who'd never been married, a man who professed to hate children, have all these things? Questions whirled in her head as she walked over to the crib and stared at it in bewilderment.

"What in the hell are you doing in here?"

She gasped in surprise and whirled around to see Jack standing in the doorway, the fires of rage burning in his eyes.

Jack knew his rage was out of proportion for the offense, but this room held all his dashed hopes, all his broken dreams and every heartache he possessed.

He hadn't been in it for months and certainly hadn't wanted to share it with anyone else.

"I—I thought this was the bathroom. I'm sorry." She took a step back from him, her eyes wary.

The initial rage seeped out of him and he nodded curtly. "The bathroom is across the hall."

He was vaguely aware of her slipping past him and disappearing from the room.

Being in this room was like being thrust back in time…a time when a dark-haired child had laughed and grinned from the crib, a little boy who had called him Daddy, who had given him sloppy kisses and captured his heart.

He walked over to the toddler bed, bought for a third birthday and never slept in. The fire truck was for a fourth birthday, the baseball mitt for a fifth. Stuffed animals, clothing progressing in sizes… Christmas presents never opened, a future never realized.

Jack was unaware of the passing of time as he stood in the room and stared at the items that would never be played with, never be worn.

He wasn't sure why he still continued to buy birthday presents and holiday surprises for a child he'd lost.

A stack of picture books rested on top of the chest of drawers. Jack had read those books to a wiggling, giggling two-year-old. They were the last presents Bobby had ever used.

The ringing of the doorbell echoed through the

house and pulled Jack from the inertia that had gripped him. He backed out of the room and closed the door, shutting in the past...and hopefully the pain.

He opened the front door to see the Chinese food deliveryman, and realized he must have been in the bedroom for some time. He paid for the order and carried it into the kitchen.

Marissa had set the table and now stood at the window, her back to him.

"I hope you're hungry." Jack forced an unnatural cheer into his voice. She turned to face him. "I ordered enough food for ten people." He began setting out containers, aware of her gaze intent on him.

He sank into a chair and motioned for her to sit opposite him. He released a weary sigh. "Don't worry, I'm not a pervert or anything like that."

"That never crossed my mind." Her eyes, so green and clear, showed her confusion, but he had a feeling if he offered no explanation, said nothing about the room she'd seen, she would respect his privacy and not mention it, either.

"His name was Bobby." The words fell unbidden from him, and in simply saying the sweet name, memories rushed in to ache inside him. "He was almost three years old the last time I saw him."

"He was your son?" she asked softly.

He nodded, although claiming Bobby as his son seemed far too simple for what the child had meant to him. Bobby had filled his world, had been the catalyst for hope and dreams.

"What happened?" Again her voice was soft. "Did...did he pass away?" Her voice held dread for his answer.

"No...at least, not that I know of." He leaned back in his chair and sighed once again. "Although there are days I think it would have been easier if he'd died. Then at least there would be some closure."

A tiny frown wrinkled the center of Marissa's forehead. "I don't understand. What happened?"

Jack took a moment to open the lid of several of the Chinese food containers on the table. He had spent the past year trying desperately not to think about Sherry, about Bobby, shoving away the pain, swallowing the grief.

"I met Sherry, Bobby's mother, while I was still a cop. There had been a break-in at her apartment and I was the one who caught the call. Sherry was beautiful and lively and there was an instant attraction between us. Almost immediately we started a relationship and within two months, she was pregnant." He pushed one of the containers toward Marissa.

"No, thanks," she said. "I'll eat later."

He wasn't hungry at the moment, either. "I begged Sherry to marry me, but she wanted nothing to do with marriage, said things were happening too fast, that we needed to slow down. Still, she moved in here with me when she was five months pregnant and on April fifth, Bobby was born.''

For a moment, sweet memories rushed through him as he thought of the instant his son had come into the world, lustily squalling and waving his tiny hands like a prizefighter.

"Bobby weighed seven pounds six ounces and had a full head of dark hair. I thought he was the most beautiful child ever born.'' He raked his hand through his hair and continued, "Every day I asked Sherry to marry me, but she kept refusing. I thought it was important that we get married, but she didn't see it that way.''

Jack got up and walked to the window where Marissa had been standing when he'd first come into the kitchen. He stared out unseeing, his mind's eye focused on the distant past.

"I knew Sherry wasn't happy, had begun to realize she was a better lover than mother. She said she hated my job, so I quit the force and became an investigator. I figured maybe if I was home more often, things would be okay. But she was restless, went out most evenings while I baby-sat Bobby. I knew things were going to change, but I was determined that no matter what happened with me and Sherry, I would remain a big part of Bobby's life. One morning I kissed her and Bobby goodbye, and when I got home from work that evening, they were gone.''

"Oh, Jack.''

He turned from the window and faced Marissa, saw the sympathy that darkened her eyes and softened her features. "She left me a note, told me it was time for her to move on, that the routine was getting to her. She told me not to try to find them."

"Did you?"

"Did I try to find them?" A sharp, bitter laugh exploded from him. "I did nothing else. I spent every waking moment, used every resource I could think of, but it was like the air had swallowed them whole."

"And how long ago was that?"

"Five years ago. Three years ago I found out that Sherry was killed in a car accident in Miami and Bobby was swallowed up in the system."

"What do you mean?" She stood and took a step toward him.

"Apparently the state took Bobby and placed him in foster care. I contacted a social worker in Miami, but it turned out to be a dead end. The official record showed that Bobby was listed as 'father unknown.'"

Bitterness tore through him. "That's when I discovered Sherry hadn't even listed me as the father on his birth records. Legally, I have no rights to him at all."

"So, what happened?"

"What happened? I came back here and waited for the social worker to contact me. I hounded her, but kept getting the runaround. So I spent the next year drunk, and then about a year ago I got tired of getting drunk.'' He shrugged his shoulders. ''And that's the end of my sad story.''

He suddenly was exhausted, as if the telling of his past had both physically and mentally depleted him. His leg and his hand ached more acutely than they had in the past two days.

''And the things in the bedroom?'' she asked.

''Stuff for Bobby. Every April fifth, every Christmas I buy something for him. I don't know why I do it. It's some sort of perverse compulsion,'' he confessed.

Marissa moved closer to him and reached up and placed her palms on his cheeks. Her hands were warm and her gaze held his. She stood so close to him her breasts pressed into his chest and her body heat warmed him.

''I'm so sorry, Jack. I can't imagine loving then losing a child.'' Her breath was warm on his face, her lips so close that if he bent his head slightly he could capture them with his own.

''And I hope you never experience it,'' he replied. The pain the assault of memories had evoked lessened as desire stirred inside him.

He knew she was attempting to comfort him, and he wanted to fall into that comfort, allow his desire for her to sweep away the last of his pain. Without hesitation, he lowered his mouth to hers.

Chapter Six

Marissa had wanted to comfort, but as Jack's mouth came crashing down to hers, the need to comfort was swept away by an even stronger emotion.

He gave her no chance to breathe, no opportunity to think as his lips plied hers with a hungry heat. His arms encircled her and drew her more intimately against him.

She placed her hands on his chest, thinking she might push against him to protest the kiss. But of their own volition her arms moved her hands up from his chest to wrap around his neck and her fingers played across the breadth and strength of his shoulders. Helplessly, she gave in to the sensual assault.

Someplace in the back of her mind she realized

she'd wanted Jack to kiss her, had known that he would kiss with passion and depth. She hadn't been mistaken.

He deepened the kiss, his tongue entering her mouth and swirling with hers. At the same time the fingers of his good hand moved beneath her T-shirt to caress the bare skin of her lower back.

The gentle warm touch on her skin, coupled with the fire in his kiss, shot a sweet heat of desire through her. Her head filled with the scent of him, the masculine fragrance of cologne and soap.

Jack Coffey might not be her Mr. Right, but he definitely knew how to kiss.

His mouth finally left hers and trailed down the side of her neck. She knew the smart thing to do would be to step back, distance herself from his bewitching touch, the magic of his lips.

However, she didn't want to be smart, and she didn't want to distance herself. She wasn't even sure if she was physically capable of stepping back, with her legs so weak and her body trembling with desire.

She dropped her head back, allowing him access to the hollow of her throat. She tangled her hands in his hair, vaguely surprised to find it silky soft.

"Marissa," he whispered against her ear, then captured the lobe in his mouth. "I want you."

The words, husky and filled with desire, sent a shiver of excitement racing up her spine. But along with the shiver came the first whisper of common sense and rationality.

She could allow herself to fall completely into the spell of desire he was weaving around her, throw caution to the wind and let him make sweet love to her. But what could possibly come of it?

At best, he'd be a vacation memory to take home with her, an unwanted souvenir of passion spent with Mr. Wrong. He wasn't her Mr. Right, and she wasn't about to make a mistake as she had with Bill.

Besides, their emotions had been running high just before the kiss. She didn't trust that what Jack felt for her, what she was feeling at the moment, was true.

They had known each other for only a couple of days. This whole thing was madness...sheer madness.

"Jack..." She pushed gently against his chest.

He released her immediately and stepped back from her. "Sorry." His eyes blazed with blue flames. "It's been a while since I've held a woman in my arms. I allowed myself to get out of control. It won't happen again."

He sat at the table and began to serve himself some food from the containers. Marissa sat, too, her body still tingling from the sensations he'd stirred inside her.

"It's been a while since I've been held by a man," she said. "I allowed myself to get a little out of control, as well."

He handed her a container of sweet and sour

chicken. "You haven't been with anyone since Nathaniel's father?"

She felt a blush warm her cheeks. "No." She couldn't help herself—she had to ask. "What about you?"

"There've been a few ships passing in my nights, but not many and not for a long while. Finding women who understand the score is difficult."

"The score? What do you mean?"

He speared a piece of chicken with a chopstick and chewed thoughtfully before replying. The blaze in his eyes was gone, leaving them a familiar cold, cynical blue.

"Most women want the whole routine—candlelight dinners, soulful glances filled with meaning, sweet words that mean nothing and, worst of all, commitment. All I'm interested in is a healthy physical interaction with no emotional strings attached."

If Marissa had entertained any regret at stopping their kisses and caresses, that regret fell away beneath his words. His statement of what he was looking for underscored the enormous differences between them.

She liked Jack, and she was incredibly physically drawn to him, but she would never be a ship passing in the night with him. She knew her body and her heart were intricately tied together, and making love for her was far more than mere physical interaction.

For a few minutes they ate silently. As Marissa

enjoyed the excellent food, she worked to process everything she'd learned about Jack.

He'd had a son...a son he'd obviously loved and lost. Her heart ached for his loss. There were times when Nathaniel could be a pain, when he got cranky and wasn't as pleasant to be around, but Marissa couldn't imagine her life without him.

To love a child, as Jack obviously had, for almost three years. To watch a child grow from baby to toddler, see him learn and experience new things, to hold him, then to lose him had to be beyond wrenching.

A cry from Nathaniel interrupted both Marissa's thoughts and their meal. She excused herself from the table and went into the living room to see Nathaniel sitting up and rubbing his eyes.

"Hey, big guy," she greeted him, and he grinned and raised his arms for her to pick him up. She grabbed him to her chest and hugged him tightly, empathy for Jack's loss slicing through her.

Nathaniel squealed his displeasure at her too-tight embrace and she eased her hold on him.

"I'll bet you're hungry." She carried him into the kitchen and placed him in a chair between hers and Jack's.

"Does he eat Chinese?" Jack asked, the familiar scowl once again on his face.

"He eats almost anything." Marissa returned to her chair and handed Nathaniel a piece of sweet and sour chicken. He took a bite and grinned at Jack as if to prove his wide range of culinary experience.

"Just don't give him a chopstick," Jack said. "I shudder at the thought of what damage he could do."

Marissa started to make a teasing retort, but one look at Jack's face stopped her. Silence fell between them. Jack wore his scowl like a shield of defense, as if daring her to breach the wall of silence he'd erected.

And again, as the silence lengthened, Marissa found herself thinking about his little boy. According to what Jack had told her, she calculated that Bobby would now be almost eight years old.

She couldn't imagine what had driven Sherry to cut Jack out of her son's life, nor could she imagine why the woman hadn't named him as Bobby's father on the birth certificate. She guessed that Jack didn't want to pursue the subject, but she couldn't help herself. She wanted to know more. "Jack?"

He looked at her, his gaze wary. "What?"

"Why didn't Sherry put you on the birth certificate? Is it possible Bobby isn't your child?"

She was almost sorry she'd asked, as pain immediately darkened his eyes. She thought for a moment he was going to get angry, tell her to mind her own business and get out of his house. Instead, he set down his fork, took a sip of his drink and frowned thoughtfully.

"Bobby is my child. I'm absolutely certain of

that. Everyone commented on how much alike we looked. Other than Bobby getting Sherry's brown eyes instead of my blue ones, he was the spitting image of me.''

"So, why didn't she put you on the birth certificate?"

He took another sip of his water and leaned back in his chair, the same thoughtful frown remaining on his face. "I'm not sure. I can't know what was going on in her mind at that time, but I've done a lot of speculating."

"More." Nathaniel held out a sticky hand for more chicken.

Marissa gave him another piece, then focused her attention back to Jack. "And what have you speculated?"

"I think Sherry knew at the time of Bobby's birth that she didn't intend to stay with me. I think she left my name off the certificate so there would be no legal ties, no hassle over custody, nothing to bind her to me."

"But wouldn't she have wanted Bobby to know, to have a relationship with his father?"

Jack smiled, but it was a gesture void of humor. "I don't like to talk ill of the dead, but the fact is Sherry could be extremely selfish. She wouldn't consider what was in Bobby's best interest, only what was in her own best interest. She didn't like hassles of any kind, and sharing custody of Bobby would have been a hassle."

"How sad." Marissa looked at Nathaniel and sighed. "It seems unfair that you want to be a father and can't find your son, and I have a son whose father wants nothing to do with him."

A cynical smile curved Jack's lips. "Haven't you figured out yet that life isn't fair, that love doesn't conquer all and dreams are merely fantasies life gives you to make you want what will never come true?"

"You can't really believe all that," Marissa replied, shocked by the vehemence in his words. She pushed her plate aside, finished with her meal and focused all her attention on the man across from her.

"You have to believe that eventually there will be a happy ending for you and Bobby, that you'll find him and be reunited."

"I quit looking for him two years ago."

"Why?" Marissa asked incredulously.

Jack stood and carried his plate to the sink. "Because it was no use," he replied with his back to her. "Nobody could tell me anything and I was just spinning my wheels."

He turned to face her, bitterness razing her from his gaze. "I'm the best private investigator in the entire state—my expertise is finding missing people—but I can't find my own son."

"But, Jack—" Marissa stood and carried her plate to where he stood. "There have been so many advances in the past two years as far as networking and record keeping go. You need to go back to Miami, start the process of looking for Bobby all over again.''

"You can be a Pollyanna in your own life, but don't try to make me one.''

If tone of voice had the power to kill, Marissa would have been dead on the spot. She recognized his utter hopelessness and wanted to wrap him in her arms, hold him until he found something positive to believe in.

But of course, that would be foolishness. Jack Coffey meant nothing to her. It shouldn't matter to her if he remained for the rest of his life the most bitter, unhappy and lonely man in the world.

It shouldn't matter to her if he entertained hope or believed in love, or possessed secret dreams. It shouldn't matter, yet the emptiness in his eyes, the cold scorn in his voice tore through her heart. It shouldn't matter...but it did.

"Look, Marissa.'' Jack swiped a hand through his hair, his gaze not meeting hers. "You've been an enormous help to me for the past couple of days. You typed up my reports, cooked me a meal and drove me to my stakeout. Why don't we call it even and you get back to your vacation and I'll get back to my life.''

"Sounds like a good plan to me,'' Marissa replied. It was obvious to her that he was ready for her to exit his life. She certainly didn't intend to remain where she wasn't wanted or needed.

She pushed back Nathaniel's chair and picked

him up in her arms. He squealed a lusty protest, but she ignored him. He was probably not finished eating, but she'd grab a hamburger or something for him on their way back to the motel.

"Don't forget his diaper bag," Jack said, his expression unreadable.

"Don't worry," Marissa replied dryly. "I'll make sure I don't have a reason to come back." She turned and left the kitchen and went into the living room. She grabbed Nathaniel's blanket and diaper bag from the floor, then started for the door.

"Marissa?"

She turned from the door and gazed at Jack. "I hope you enjoy the rest of your vacation," he said.

"I have every intention of doing just that." She slipped out the door and down the stairs to her car.

Marissa settled Nathaniel in his car seat, then got behind the wheel and started the engine. Only when Jack's house had disappeared from sight in her rearview mirror did she acknowledge the ache in her heart.

Surely her heart hurt only because as a nurse's aide she was trained to help people. But as a nurse's aide, she'd recognized long ago that there were some people too sick to be helped. And she suspected Jack was one of those people.

Although not plagued by a physical illness, Jack suffered a soul sickness just as devastating and even more difficult to treat.

Besides, Jack wasn't one of her patients. He was

nothing more than a man she'd met on her vacation, a man who had taken up less than a week of her time. She was certain she wouldn't see or hear from him again, but she had a terrible feeling that thoughts of him would haunt her for a long time to come.

Jack had always been comfortable in the silence of his house. He wasn't a man who turned on the television or a radio to fill the silence. But the moment Marissa and Nathaniel left, the quiet of the house pressed against him with suffocating intensity.

He cleaned up the kitchen, stuffed the leftover Chinese food in the refrigerator, then grabbed a glass of iced tea and went out on his deck.

The midafternoon sun was hot, but felt good. He sat in one of the chairs and propped his feet in the other as he stared out to the breaking waves of water.

Bobby had loved the water…loved the outdoors. Even when he'd been a tiny baby, when he'd been fussy, all Jack had had to do was bring him out here, and the breeze wafting off the water and the rhythmic sound of the waves would calm him.

Bobby. Damn Marissa Criswell for stirring up the past, for reminding him of all he'd lost. He'd been doing just fine before she'd stepped into that bedroom. He'd finally managed to put the pain aside, move on and come to terms with losing Bobby.

Now, however, as he stared out at the water, his

pain came in mirroring waves, sweeping through him with drowning intensity.

If his leg wasn't in a cast, he'd go jogging on the beach. He would have run until he was too tired to think, too exhausted to feel. Unfortunately, at the moment that wasn't an option.

Instead, he closed his eyes, deciding that if he didn't look at the waves breaking onto the shore, perhaps he'd stop thinking about Bobby.

It worked. Almost instantly his head filled with the memory of the kiss he'd shared with Marissa. As he remembered the sweet taste of her lips, the feel of her breasts against his chest, the heat of the sun overhead seemed to intensify.

He'd known instinctively that kissing her would be pleasant. What he hadn't expected was the raw passion, the overwhelming desire that had devoured him as he'd held her in his arms.

Surely his desire for her came solely from the fact that it had been a long time since he'd been with a woman. Surely it had nothing to do with the be-witching freckles that danced across her nose and her eyes that invited a man to drown in them.

His desire for her couldn't be because she pos-sessed a wit that rivaled his own and made him laugh as he couldn't remember laughing in a long time. It couldn't be because that humor was quickly replaced by the ferocity of a lion where her son was concerned.

He missed them. They'd been gone from his

house only an hour, but he felt their absence. They'd swept into his life, bringing chaos and laughter, and now they were gone.

He opened his eyes and once again stared at the breaking waves. It was good that they were gone. He didn't need a freckle-faced Pollyanna and her killer kid around.

The afternoon and early-evening hours crept by slowly. Jack made a couple of phone calls, putting off the cases he could until he was more mobile.

He received a phone call telling him that Samuel Jacobson had agreed to pay all back child support to his wife and that the transfer of funds had already been accomplished.

Jack ate leftover Chinese food for supper, then sat on the sofa and turned on the television, unable to stand the pressing silence of the house any longer.

After watching two sitcoms, he realized why he rarely watched television. The sitcoms were stupid and the canned laughter irritated him.

He turned off the set and once again the silence settled around him. Why did it bother him so much now when it never had before? He didn't even want to think of what the answer might be.

He finally gave up and went to bed, falling instantly into a restless sleep. He slept late the next morning and was seated at the kitchen table drinking a cup of coffee when a knock resounded at his door.

Eagerly Jack struggled to his feet. She must have thought of some reason to come back. He flung open the door, knowing he wore an expectant smile. Instead of Marissa and Nathaniel, Maria stood at his door.

The disappointment that shot through him irritated him. "What are you doing here?" he snapped. "I figured by now you would have taken your bingo winnings and left the country." He stepped aside to allow her entry.

"I would never leave the country without making sure you were taken care of first," Maria protested.

Jack raised an eyebrow in disbelief. "Yeah, right. How much did you lose?"

Maria walked into the kitchen, poured herself a cup of coffee and sank down at the table, her dark eyes snapping with petulance. "I was just going to play five cards, but my sister said for me to play ten. She kept telling me I was going to win. 'Before the night is over, you'll be a big winner.'" She snorted and whirled a hand through her gray hair. "My sister, the psychic. More like my sister, the psycho."

Despite his former foul mood, Jack laughed and sat in the chair across from her.

She sat back, as if surprised by his burst of laughter. "Now, that's a rare sound in this house." She snapped her eyes closed. "I'm getting a vision."

"I thought your sister was the psycho," Jack replied dryly.

She cracked open an eyelid. "It runs in our family. Anyway...I have a vision of a woman with short blond hair and long legs. She has a little boy...a little blond boy with dancing blue eyes. I think they have brought laughter back into this house.''

For an instant, Jack was astonished by her words, then he remembered that on the morning he'd fired Maria she had been going out when Marissa had been coming in.

''Wait...I'm getting a vision of my own,'' Jack replied. ''I see a bingo-losing, nosy housekeeper groveling to her former employer to get her job back.''

''Ha, I guess that proves we're both fakes.''

''So, are you coming back to work for me?''

Maria's gray eyebrows danced up on her forehead. ''You are giving me a raise?''

''Nope. Not this time. I already pay you twice what the going rate is for housecleaning.''

''But I'm worth every penny.''

Jack laughed, wondering how he'd managed to surround himself with mouthy women. First Maria, then Marissa. Both women were stubborn, opinionated and filled with faith. Maria just knew that any day she was going to win the Lotto or win big at bingo. Her faith in big winnings was as devout as Marissa's was in finding Mr. Right.

''I don't grovel,'' Maria said indignantly. ''But if you want, I could work for you right now. My supplies are in the car.'' She rose from the sofa.

''That'll work,'' Jack agreed. ''I'm going to pack

up a few things in Bobby's room, so make sure you dust and vacuum in there.''

Maria looked at him in surprise. That room was usually off-limits to everyone, including her. "Okay, then I'll be right back.''

Jack remained seated as Maria let herself out the door. He'd vaguely surprised himself with his statement about packing up things in Bobby's room. But he realized now the idea had been floating around in the back of his head for most of the morning.

He pulled himself to his feet and went to Bobby's bedroom. He saw the toys that would never be played with, the clothing that would now be too small to wear.

There was really no reason to hang on to the stuff. Jack knew that on Bobby's birth date he would go out and buy something appropriate for an eight-year-old. He would continue to add to the collection, but there was really no reason to hang on to the stuff Bobby would have already outgrown.

Might as well give it to somebody who could put it to use, he thought. He picked up a small blue sweater with a denim collar and pockets. It was just about the right size for the terminator. A smile curved his mouth as he thought of Nathaniel.

He wasn't sure when it had happened, but somehow the kid had gotten under his skin. There was little in the blue-eyed, blond boy to remind him of Bobby, so Jack knew his growing affection for Nathaniel had nothing to do with transference of affections from his own son to a child like his son.

Nathaniel was simply Nathaniel. He placed the sweater back on the toddler bed, then went to the closet to look for an empty box.

When he finished boxing up the items, he'd call Marissa and tell her to come and get them.

He steadfastly refused to acknowledge how his heart leapt with the idea of seeing her one last time.

Chapter Seven

Marissa awakened with the dawn. With Nathaniel still sleeping in the crib, she quietly got up and made coffee in the coffeemaker the motel provided. As she waited for the brew to finish, she washed and dressed.

Minutes later, with a cup of coffee in hand, she peered out the window and tried to decide how to spend the day. The sun was already peeking over the horizon, promising another warm, cloudless day, but lazing on the beach held little appeal.

She and Nathaniel had spent the whole day yesterday at the beach, playing in the sand, building castles and frolicking at the water's edge. The fresh air and sunshine had exhausted them both and they'd come back to their room, cleaned up and gone to bed early.

Maybe sight-seeing, she thought and took a sip of her coffee. Although the small town of Mason Bridge didn't particularly cater to tourists, she'd seen several shops that had looked interesting and demanded further exploration.

Jack.

His image filled her head and a tiny surge of regret swept through her as she thought of the way they had parted. He'd been angry and she'd been offended, and she wished they had parted on more amicable terms.

She frowned, steadfastly attempting to shove thoughts of him away. There was nothing to gain by entertaining thoughts of him.

She would finish her vacation, then go home and get back to her life. Jack had been an interesting diversion, but nothing more. He had been her very own ship passing in the night.

She managed to avoid thinking about Jack all day, as she and Nathaniel drove around the small town. It was just after two when they returned to their motel room. Almost immediately Nathaniel went down for a nap and Marissa unloaded the bags of items she had purchased.

She'd found a beautifully decorated trinket box for her grandmother, who collected them. She'd bought herself an oversize nightshirt that read Mason Bridge Beach. She only hoped sleeping in the shirt wouldn't evoke dreams of a certain dark-haired, blue-eyed grouch.

After tucking the trinket box into a padded compartment of her suitcase, she decided to give her grandmother a quick call and tell her again how grateful she was for the gift of the vacation.

As she sat on the edge of the bed and reached for the phone, she saw the message light blinking. She pressed the buttons to retrieve the message and was surprised to hear Jack's voice.

"Marissa…it's me. Jack…Jack Coffey. Uh… could you give me a call?" The message ended with him reciting his phone number.

Marissa committed the number to memory, but hesitated before dialing it. Why had he called? Was it possible she'd left something at his place? She ran through a quick mental checklist, but couldn't think of what she might possibly have left behind.

So why had he called? He'd sounded ill at ease, hesitant, so unlike himself.

"There's only one way to find out what he wants," she said aloud, and quickly punched in his number. "Jack," she said when he answered. "It's me."

"Hi, Marissa."

She tried to ignore the slight flutter of her heart at the sound of his deep voice. Heartburn, she told herself, probably from the burritos at lunch. "I got your message. What's up?"

"I've got something for you and I was wondering if you could come by and get it."

"Something for me?" She frowned, wondering what it could be.

"It's not a big deal," he added hurriedly. "Just a little something I thought you might be able to use. So, can you come and get it?"

"You mean right now?" She looked at the sleeping Nathaniel. "Nathaniel is taking a nap right now, so it will have to be some time later this afternoon."

There was a long pause. "Why don't you come for supper? I think I've got a couple of steaks in the freezer and can manage cooking them up...unless you have other plans."

"No, no other plans," she said quickly. She was confused. Day before yesterday, he'd all but thrown her out of his place. Now suddenly he wanted to cook her a steak dinner?

"Why don't you and junior come by about six? I'll grill a hot dog for him."

"Okay, then, I'll see you at six."

Marissa hung up, as confused as ever. She almost felt as if Jack had asked her for a date. But that was ridiculous.

Still, that evening as she got ready to go to Jack's, she felt as if she were dressing for a date. She put on and took off half a dozen outfits before finally settling on a light pink sundress that was casual, yet more dressy than shorts.

A touch of mascara, a dab of lipstick and a spritz of perfume later, she proclaimed herself ready to go. With Nathaniel clad in navy shorts and shirt and with diaper bag in hand, she got into her car and headed for Jack's place.

As she drove the short distance, she tried to still the anticipation that beat in her heart. Jack Coffey was a hopeless pessimist, a grouch and, worst of all, a man without hope…without dreams.

However, she knew it would have been easier to write him off as such had she not learned the reason he'd become such a man.

Despite his many faults, Marissa liked the man. But she refused to allow her feelings about him to deepen.

Her Mr. Right wouldn't be crabby and he wouldn't be a man without hope. She'd tried to make Bill into her Mr. Right, but it hadn't worked. She didn't intend to go through the same futility in trying to transform Jack Coffey into her Mr. Right.

When her Mr. Right entered her life she would know in an instant, and she wouldn't have to worry about changing him. He'd be perfect already.

However, she couldn't explain the sweet anticipation that rushed through her as his house came into view. She couldn't explain the flutter of excitement that rippled through her as she thought of seeing him once again.

"Daddy," Nathaniel said as she pulled him from his car seat and started up the steps to Jack's door.

"No. Jack," Marissa corrected her son.

Nathaniel laughed and pointed to the door. "Daddy," he repeated.

Marissa frowned as she knocked on the door. She wasn't going to argue with a two-year-old, but this daddy fixation Nathaniel had developed worried her a little.

Jack opened the door and her breath caught slightly in her throat. Never had he looked more handsome than at the moment. He was clean shaven, with his hair neatly combed. He was dressed in a pair of navy slacks, one leg cut off to accommodate the bulk of the cast, and a pale blue short-sleeved shirt that emphasized the azure depths of his eyes. He'd apparently given up the crutches altogether now, relying on the walking cast.

"Right on time," he said, and opened the door more fully to let her in.

She was greeted by the scents of window cleaner and furniture polish, and as they entered the living room it was obvious the place had been thoroughly vacuumed and cleaned. "The place looks great," she said in surprise.

"Maria came yesterday," he replied.

Marissa set Nathaniel on the floor. "Did you have to give her a raise?"

Jack grinned. "No, I got lucky. She lost her shirt at bingo and was properly contrite in her return. Come on into the kitchen."

She took Nathaniel's hand and together the three of them went into the kitchen, where it was obvious Jack had been in the midst of making a salad.

Marissa opened the diaper bag and handed Nathaniel several of his toys. He plopped down on the floor, seemingly content.

"Why don't you let me do that," she said, gesturing to the salad fixings.

"Okay," he agreed. "I have to confess, wielding a knife one-handed was making me a little nervous. How about a glass of wine?"

"That sounds great," she agreed. There was a stiff formality between them that had not existed before, and Marissa wasn't sure what had caused it.

"Here you are." He set a glass of red wine next to where she was chopping green peppers. "The potatoes are already baking on the grill and the charcoal is just about ready for the steaks."

"Sounds good," she said. "When I finish with the salad do you want me to set the table?"

"I've already done that. I thought we'd eat on the deck."

Marissa nodded. She finished chopping the peppers and added them to the salad he'd already prepared. "Anything else?" she asked, knife poised in her hand.

"Nope. That should do it. Why don't we move to the deck and I'll get the steaks cooking."

"All right," she agreed.

It took them three trips to get everything they needed from the kitchen to the deck. But finally they settled in, Marissa in a chair at the table, Jack standing before the grill and Nathaniel sitting on the deck amid his favorite toys.

"How do you like your steaks?" Jack asked.

"Medium well." She took a sip of her wine, trying to figure out why the air felt thick between them, why they were acting like strangers who knew nothing about each other.

Something had changed between them, and that change filled her with a nervous tension she hadn't felt with him before.

She took another sip of her wine and studied him as he tended the steaks on the grill. Was the tension coming from him? Because she had learned the secrets of his past? The source of his pain?

She knew he'd shared the information about Sherry and Bobby only with great reluctance and probably would never have shared it with her had she not accidentally stepped into that bedroom.

She frowned thoughtfully. Still, she didn't believe that was the reason for the underlying tension.

The steaks sizzled and the air filled with the scent of cooking meat. Jack left the grill and eased down in the chair next to her. As he did, his leg brushed against hers, and suddenly Marissa knew what had caused the change between them.

The kiss.

Her mind exploded with the memory of his mouth on hers…hot…hungry…demanding. That kiss had stirred her to the depths of her soul, stirred her as no other kiss she'd ever experienced before.

She realized in an instant that it wasn't uneasiness she was feeling—it was tension. Raw sexual tension.

Every nerve she possessed tingled and she couldn't get the memory of that kiss out of her head.

And what really bothered her was the fact that she desperately hoped he would kiss her again before the night was over.

She not only had freckles across the bridge of her nose, but also possessed a splattering of flirtatious freckles on her chest. Jack noticed them as she leaned forward to pat Nathaniel on the head.

The movement exposed not only her freckles, but also a flash of cleavage and the rounded curves of the top of her breasts. For a moment Jack had a lot in common with the steak on the grill. He felt himself sizzling.

Kissing her two days before had been a huge mistake. No matter how hard he tried, he couldn't get the taste of her out of his mouth, couldn't get the feel of her warm curves pressed tightly against him out of his head.

He focused his attention on the steaks, wondering what madness had prompted his invitation for dinner. All he'd meant to do was have her come by to get the box of Bobby's things that Nathaniel might use. But when she'd called him, he'd found himself extending the dinner invitation.

He turned the steaks with a frown. It had been easier than he'd thought it would be to pack up some of the things in Bobby's room. As he'd packed them up, memories had engulfed him…sweet memories of loving Bobby, of being loved by Bobby.

At first he'd fought those memories, unwanted treasures from a time that no longer existed. Finally he'd simply given in to them and was surprised that although there was pain attached to the remembrances of Bobby, there was also incredible joy.

Somewhere in the past months, a healing of sorts had occurred. Although his heart would always ache for the child he had lost, the pain was slowly becoming manageable.

"You're very quiet," Marissa said. "Is your leg hurting you? Maybe it's too soon to be walking on it."

"No, it's feeling all right." He slapped the cast. "I guess I was just concentrating on getting these steaks cooked just right."

She smiled, and the warmth of her smile shot heat through him. "It's been my experience that you can't screw up a good steak."

"You'd be surprised what I can do when attempting to cook."

"You're that bad?" Her eyes twinkled merrily.

"Terrible, the absolute worst," He grinned. "Dogs don't mess with my garbage because they're afraid it might be filled with the leftovers of meals I've cooked."

She laughed, picked up her wineglass, then left the table and joined him at the grill. "Maybe I'd better supervise, just to be on the safe side."

She stood close enough to him that despite the aroma of the barbecuing meat, he could smell the scent of her. He was intensely aware of her as he hadn't been of a woman for a very long time.

Oh, yes, kissing her had been a definite mistake. Before the kiss, she'd been nothing more than a cheerful irritant, a necessary helpmate. But at the moment all he could think about was the fact that she was a very attractive woman who kissed with a heat and passion that had moved him.

"Jack, you better flip them."

Her voice pulled him from his thoughts and he stared at her blankly.

"The steaks…they're starting to burn."

He flipped them quickly, aware of her gaze lingering on him.

"Are you sure you're all right?" she asked, a worried frown crinkling the center of her forehead.

"I'm fine," he assured her. "Just a little distracted."

"Thinking about one of your cases?" The frown in her forehead deepened. "You know, if you need me to drive you someplace, or help you type some more reports, I'll be happy to help."

"No, I've taken advantage of you long enough." He added a hot dog to the grill, then looked at her. "I've played on your guilt over what was nothing more than a hapless accident."

She smiled. "You couldn't have played on my guilt because I didn't feel guilty. However, I did feel somewhat responsible.'' She cast a quick glance at her son. ''I should have kept a better eye on Nathaniel. Usually he's a pretty sedentary child. He usually stays wherever I put him. I don't know what possessed him to wander away that day at the beach.''

Jack looked at Nathaniel, who was seated on the deck floor and seemed perfectly content with the building blocks that surrounded him. ''Yeah, he does seem to sit better than most kids his age.''

''In my experience there are two kinds of two-year-olds, the explorers and the thinkers. Nathaniel is a thinker.'' She tilted her head to one side, her eyes the soft green of newly budded leaves. ''What kind was Bobby?''

For just a second, Jack's defenses kicked in and he wanted to tell her it was none of her business, that it was a taboo topic and he didn't intend to discuss it.

As quickly as it came, the instinct disappeared. For five long years he hadn't talked about Bobby with anyone. Other than on Bobby's birthday and various holidays, Jack had pretended Bobby didn't exist—had never existed—because it made it easier.

Suddenly, for the first time since the day Sherry had taken Bobby away, Jack wanted to talk about the son he'd lost.

''Bobby was an explorer, into everything.'' Jack removed the steaks and the hot dog from the grill.

"You couldn't turn your back on him for a minute," he continued as they settled at the table to eat.

"My sister has a child like that," Marissa said as she cut Nathaniel's hot dog into bite-size pieces.

Jack eyed her curiously. "How many brothers and sisters do you have?"

"One younger sister."

"And is she an eternal optimist like you?" he teased.

"She's even worse than me." Marissa laughed, and again Jack felt a warmth fill his chest and seep toward his extremities. "Sandra married her high school sweetheart and they've built a wonderful life together. They love each other passionately and they're both utterly mad about their two children."

She had a soft, dreamy look on her face and Jack knew she was imagining her Mr. Right and the life she would build with him.

For a brief moment, envy swept through him as he thought of the man who would eventually possess Marissa's love, the man who would get to spend his life laughing with her, loving her.

"It must be genetic," he replied, irritated with himself for his crazy thoughts.

She laughed. "I think you possess a few flaws of your own, Jack Coffey."

He winced. "Please, let's not get into those."

"You don't talk about my flaws, and I won't talk about yours," she said.

He grinned. "It's a deal."

The rest of the meal progressed pleasantly. As the sun slowly sank on the horizon, Jack talked about some of his previous cases, exaggerating humorous elements just to hear the rich music of her laughter.

And he spoke of Bobby. He told her how the little boy had loved the sound of the ocean waves, how he'd liked to have his belly tickled and would dance to any music. It was both pleasure and pain to talk of him, but Jack shoved aside the pain and immersed himself in the joy those memories brought to mind, to heart.

Nathaniel ate his hot dog, then pointed to Jack's plate. "More," he said.

"Here, Nathaniel, you can have some of mine." Marissa cut some of her potato off and placed it on her son's plate.

"No." Nathaniel shook his head and again pointed to Jack's plate. "Daddy more."

Daddy. As always, the word pierced Jack's heart.

"Nathaniel, what do you want?" Marissa asked. "You want some steak?" She quickly cut tiny pieces and added them to the piece of potato on Nathaniel's plate.

"No," Nathaniel repeated, this time more forcefully. "No Mommy. Daddy more."

Jack swallowed a lump of emotion. "I guess he wants some of mine." He cut off a piece of potato and put it on the boy's plate.

Nathaniel offered him a beatific smile. He reached

over and patted Jack's arm, then grabbed the piece of potato and popped it into his mouth.

Again, emotion clawed at Jack. This little boy was so needy for a father, and that neediness shone from his eyes, was displayed in the touch Nathaniel had given Jack.

In another lifetime, perhaps Jack might have been able to fulfill Nathaniel's need. But not in this one. Not with Jack so filled with memories of another child.

When Sherry had taken Bobby away, she'd also taken Jack's heart, leaving behind nothing worthwhile that might benefit anyone else.

In another lifetime, Jack might have loved Nathaniel, but in this one, Jack had no more love to give.

Chapter Eight

"I've been thinking about taking your advice and maybe contacting social services in Miami again," Jack surprised her by saying as they cleaned up the dinner dishes.

"Really?" Joy swept through Marissa at his words and all they implied. "When?"

"I don't know. Whenever I can get to Miami. I don't want to do it over the phone. It's too easy to ignore a phone call."

"I'll drive you to Miami. It's only a four-hour drive. We could go tomorrow."

He frowned. "I can't ask you to do that. This is my business, my life, and I've taken up so much of your vacation time already."

She put their plates in the dishwasher, then turned

to face him. "I don't mind, Jack. Really. Besides, I'd sort of planned a little side trip to Miami."

He eyed her dubiously. "Why would anyone plan a side trip to Miami?"

"I was going to take Nathaniel to the Seaquarium." It was kind of the truth. She'd thought about it, had read a brochure about the tourist attraction, but hadn't decided to actually make the trip.

She could tell he didn't believe her. He shook his head, then his gaze captured hers for a long moment. Gone was the cool cynicism, the hard defensiveness.

"Why are you doing this?" he asked softly. "Why are you wasting so much of your vacation time on me?"

She searched her mind for a flippant response, but none was forthcoming. *Because as crazy as it sounds, in the short time I've known you, I've come to care about you.* The words played in her head, but she knew better than to voice them aloud. "I don't know," she finally said. She forced a lightness to her voice. "Despite your many character flaws, I've enjoyed spending time with you."

He broke his gaze with her and grabbed the bowl of leftover salad. "All that proves is that you have some major flaws of your own." He covered the bowl and placed it in the refrigerator, then looked at her once again. "Sometimes I get cranky on long car trips," he warned her.

"Then you can ride in the trunk, because I don't put up with cranky passengers."

He grinned, and in that boyish smile she felt something fragile and wonderful connecting them. It confused her—both thrilled and frightened her.

He felt it, too. She could see it in his eyes, and knew that he was momentarily bathed in the same strange magic as she.

His smile fell away and a deep frown replaced it. "I'll get the stuff I have for you. I'm sure it's getting close to Nate's bedtime and you'll be wanting to get back to your motel."

"Yes, it is getting late," she replied. She picked up Nathaniel, who'd been sitting on the floor, and followed Jack into the living room.

"Wait here. I'll be right back." He disappeared down the hallway.

Marissa sat on the sofa with Nathaniel in her lap. She had never been as confused about a man as she was about Jack. He seemed to invite her closer, only to shove her away.

She cared about him. She was amazed to acknowledge it. How had Jack Coffey become so important to her in the space of so little time?

She realized that with his decision to go back to Miami and resume the search for Bobby, he'd taken a big step. If she held the power, if it was within her means, she would make certain that this search culminated in success and he would get back the son he'd lost.

But she didn't have it in her power, and his success or failure in this quest had nothing to do with her life.

In less than two weeks she'd be back in Kansas City, immersed in the daily routine of single parenting, struggling to give her son the kind of life she wanted for him.

Jack reentered the living room, gingerly carrying two large boxes.

"What's all that?" she asked.

He put the boxes down. "Take a look."

She put Nathaniel on the floor and left the sofa as Jack sat in a chair nearby. She opened up the flaps of the top box to display a variety of toys inside. She instantly recognized them. She'd seen them in Bobby's room the day before.

She looked up at Jack. "Are you sure you want to do this?"

He shrugged, his eyes dark and fathomless. "There's really no point in me keeping them around here. Even if Bobby magically appeared tomorrow, he'd be too old for that stuff."

Nathaniel stood and peered into the box, his face lighting up with delight as he saw a large fire engine. "Twuck!" He clapped his hands together with excitement as Marissa pulled the truck from the box and set it on the floor.

With Nathaniel happily occupied, Marissa moved the top box aside and opened the bottom one. Clothes. All of them still with the tags, all of them good, expensive brands.

"There's a variety of sizes, mostly twos and fours," Jack said.

"I don't know what to say…. Thank you."

Again he shrugged. "If I didn't give them to you, I'd probably box them up for charity. It was time to clean out some of that stuff."

Although his voice was light, Marissa knew the emotion that had to be ripping through him, the enormous grief that must have suffused him as he'd packed the items.

For just a moment, his grief became hers as empathetic pain washed over her. She picked up a tiny pair of jeans and ran her hand across the fabric, waiting for her emotion to become manageable.

"Maybe in Miami you'll find some answers, be able to find Bobby at last," she finally said softly.

His blue eyes grew cold. "I'm not holding my breath. I just figured I needed to make one last attempt before I finally put it all behind me."

He got up from the chair. "Unlike you, I stopped looking for happy endings a long time ago."

She knew instinctively now was not the time for any cheerleading protests to the contrary. "I know sometimes there are no happy endings, Jack. I know life is not always fair and sometimes the bad guys win." She closed the box flaps and stood.

He eyed her dubiously. "You had a bad relationship with a man who let you down when you got pregnant. What do you know about real heartache?"

Without warning, anger swept through Marissa.

"Honestly, Jack, do you really think you've cornered the market on heartache? When I was ten years old my mother died. My father was already divorced from her and a sporadic presence in our lives at best."

"You never told me that," he protested.

"Why would I? There are a lot of things you don't know about me." She raked a hand through her hair, the momentary burst of anger slowly seeping away.

"I learned very young that you have two choices in life. You either choose to be happy or you choose to be miserable. You either fight or you give up. You have to decide what kind of man you are—a survivor or a victim of life."

"You finished?" he asked, the corners of his lips curving up into a half smile.

She flushed. "I'm not sure." She offered him a small smile. "I guess for now I'm finished."

"Good. You want a cup of coffee? We could sit on the deck and enjoy a cup."

She hesitated. She would love to sit and drink coffee with him, watch the moonlight dance over the water and just spend more time with him. But the allure of the scene was almost too great... dangerously great.

"I'd better go ahead and get back to the motel," she said. "It's already almost nine, past Nathaniel's bedtime. Besides, if we're going to go to Miami tomorrow, shouldn't we get an early start?"

"Yeah, you're right," he agreed, his gaze once again inscrutable.

She looked at the boxes, then at Nathaniel who was still pushing the fire truck around the floor and making throaty noises to mimic a vehicle.

"Would you watch him while I run these boxes down to the car?"

"Yeah. Sorry I can't help."

She smiled. "That's okay. I can handle it." She picked up the first box and went out the front door. As she loaded the boxes, she tried not to think about how much she'd like to stay.

Somehow in the past twenty-four hours, her relationship with Jack had deepened, transformed from a light acquaintance to something far more meaningful.

If she were very smart, she'd run for the hills. She'd take back her offer to drive him to Miami the next day and stop seeing him altogether.

As she loaded the second box into the trunk of her car, she wondered why on earth she didn't intend to be smart.

"Mr. Coffey, do you remember the person you spoke with when you came in here before?" Barbara Klein offered Jack a hopeful smile. "It isn't necessary that I know, but it's possible I might be able to pull up some previous paperwork."

Jack frowned, trying to remember that time so long ago when he'd come here to the Miami Social

Services seeking information about his son. "Green. Her last name was Green, but I don't remember her first name."

"Elizabeth," Barbara said, supplying the missing name with a frown. "She was only with us for a short time." She pursed her lips, her frown deepening. "She had a bit of a drinking problem."

Jack laughed, the laughter tinged with a touch of bitter irony. "I guess that's why she didn't do much follow-up." Shock riveted through him as Marissa reached over and took his hand in hers.

It didn't shock him so much that she'd made the gesture. What surprised him was how welcome it felt. The warmth, the strength, the support her hand offered him sent heat straight up his arm to lodge in his heart.

The phone on the desk rang and Barbara answered. When she hung up, she smiled at them apologetically. "Something needs my attention. If you'll excuse me for a moment, I promise to be right back." She rose and left the office, softly closing the door behind her.

Jack gently pulled his hand from Marissa's and stood. "Just my luck to try to work with a woman who has a drinking problem," he said, and shook his head.

"Barbara Klein doesn't seem to have the same problem, so maybe finally you'll get some answers."

Irritation swept through Jack, an irritation he had

spent all morning trying to keep to himself. He knew exactly what was causing his irritation. Sexual frustration.

He'd spent the morning cooped up in a car with Marissa, where her scent had filled the air and her nearness had teasingly taunted him.

When he'd asked her if she wanted to share coffee with him the night before, what he'd really wanted was for her to stay the night and share coffee the next morning.

He'd wanted her to sleep in his bed, in his arms after they'd made wild, passionate love. He'd wanted to watch the morning sun spill across her face as he awakened her with hot, sweet caresses.

He flung himself back in his chair as Barbara reentered the small office.

"Now, let's get some information from you," she said to Jack. "And we'll see what I can find out."

For the next hour Jack told Barbara Klein pertinent information about his relationship with Sherry and his desire to have Bobby back in his life.

"Okay, that should do it," Barbara said. She looked at Jack for a long moment. "I realize you've waited a long time, and it was unfortunate that Elizabeth Green was your previous contact, but you understand it will take several weeks before I can tell you anything specific." She stood. "We don't just give information about our children to anyone who walks through the door."

Jack and Marissa stood as well, Nathaniel's legs

wrapped around Marissa's waist like a young cub. "Then I can expect to hear from you in the next couple of weeks?"

Barbara offered him a warm smile. "I promise."

As they left the office and walked back outside into the midafternoon Miami sun, Jack felt curiously let down. He'd known not to expect anything from this meeting, but the energy and hope he'd carried in with him were now gone.

"You okay?" Marissa asked as they got back into her car.

"Sure. Let's just hope Barbara Klein doesn't develop a drinking habit between now and the next couple of weeks."

"I don't think you need to worry about that. She seemed very professional. Maybe we should just head back to Mason Bridge," Marissa said, still looking at him. "I mean, I'm sure this has been difficult for you."

"Nonsense." He waved a hand in irritation. "We'll go to the Seaquarium as planned. Nate wants to see the fish."

He wished she'd stop looking at him like that…as if she cared, as if she worried about him. When she looked at him with those big, soft green eyes, all he could think about was taking her in his arms and kissing her until her eyes deepened, then closed with desire.

"Okay, then, the Seaquarium it is." She put the car in gear and pulled out of their parking space.

They found the tourist spot without too much trouble and spent the next two hours watching dolphins and whales perform, learning about various species of fish and eating junk food at one of the concessions.

It was just after five when they started back for Mason Bridge. For the first hour they rode in relative silence, the quiet broken occasionally by Nathaniel, who pointed out the window and went through his repertoire of words.

Once again Jack found himself fighting his desire for Marissa. He'd watched her covetously at the Seaquarium. Her laughter stirred him, her smile shot heat through him and her natural energy and enthusiasm fed him.

He stared at the window, wondering if it were possible fate had thrown Marissa Criswell into his path just to make him crazy.

"So, tell me what I don't know about you," he asked suddenly. Maybe if they talked, he could get his mind off how much he wanted to make love to her.

"Pardon me?"

"Last night you said there were things about you that you hadn't told me. So tell me now." He shifted positions in the passenger seat and tried not to notice how the evening sun lit her features with a golden glow.

She cast him a quick glance, then laughed.

''That's a pretty tall order. What exactly do you want to know?''

He wanted to know why her laughter seemed to wrap around him like a comforting blanket on a cold night. He wanted to know why the scent of her stirred him to such heights. And he wanted to know why she was so certain that he was Mr. Wrong. And knowing he wanted to know all these things scared the hell out of him.

''I don't know.... Did the grandmother who gave you this trip raise you?'' That seemed a safe enough topic.

''Yes. She took in me and my sister and made a wonderful, loving home for us. But I always felt the hole in my heart from my mother's absence.''

He nodded. Yes. That was what Bobby's absence had been—a hole in his heart. ''Nathaniel's father...did you really love him?''

She hesitated a moment before replying. ''I thought I did at the time, but I realize now I was in love with the concept of being in love. My baby sister was already happily married with two kids, I'd just finished a grueling school schedule and I was feeling lonely and isolated.''

''And then Mr. Right appeared and you knew in an instant he was the one for you.''

She heard the slight mockery in his tone and turned and stuck out her tongue. He laughed, then she continued. ''When I met Bill, I had some reservations. He ran with a bunch of guys, was heavy into the nightclub scene. He liked heavy metal music and had a stereo system in his car that could have been used as a down payment on a house.''

''Hmm, sounds like a dreamboat.''

She winced and smiled ruefully. ''I've made him sound terrible, and he wasn't all bad.'' She frowned thoughtfully. ''He made me feel pretty and wanted and not so alone, and I thought it was love, but it wasn't.''

Jack wondered if he made her feel pretty and not so alone. Was it loneliness that had made her so agreeable to spending time with him while on her vacation?

''What about you...and Sherry? You said you asked her to marry you. Were you in love with her?''

This time it was Jack's turn to contemplate that long-ago relationship. ''No,'' he confessed. ''I cared about her, and I loved her as the mother of my son, but I wasn't *in* love with her. I think she knew I wasn't in love with her, and that's why she refused to marry me.''

Again they fell silent as the car ate up the miles. Jack stared out the window, trying to sort out his conflicting emotions where Marissa was concerned.

Was it so surprising that he wanted her on a physical level? She was exceptionally attractive, with a lushness to her shape. It had been a long time since Jack had been with a woman and it was obvious he was feeling the deprivation.

He absolutely refused to consider that his desire for her might be more complicated than that.

It was just after nine when they pulled up by Jack's house. The night surrounded them and the sky was filled with a million stars.

"Why don't you come in, have that cup of coffee you didn't have last night?" Jack asked. He knew this would be the last time he would see her.

She turned off the engine and shifted in the seat to look at Nathaniel, who had fallen asleep only minutes before. He saw her hesitation. "You could carry him in and put him down in the crib."

"Okay, maybe just for a little while," she agreed.

Minutes later Jack watched from the doorway as Marissa placed the still-sleeping Nathaniel in the crib where once Bobby had slept.

Marissa kissed the little boy on the forehead, then gently covered him with a blanket. Seeing the love radiate from Marissa for her son, Jack felt an ache pierce his own heart.

Was somebody covering Bobby with a blanket right now? Kissing his forehead and making him feel safe and secure? Jack desperately hoped so. The thought of Bobby alone in the night, frightened or unhappy, tormented Jack.

He left the doorway and went into the kitchen to put the coffee on. He couldn't focus on Bobby, knew the unknowing would drive him insane.

"He didn't even crack open an eyelid," Marissa said as she came into the kitchen.

Jack nodded. "Coffee will be ready in a minute."

She looked at him for a long moment, her eyes the soft green that made him want to fall into their depths. "It must be very difficult on you to be around Nathaniel."

"I'm learning to live with the fear of bodily harm whenever I'm around him," he said, and waited for a smile to appear on her features.

She didn't smile. She simply continued to gaze at him soberly. "I'm being serious, Jack. I hadn't really thought about it until just a minute ago."

Jack got two cups from the cabinet, then turned to face her once again. "It was hard...at first," he finally admitted. "Nate is so close to the age that Bobby was when I lost him. Every time he touched me, looked at me, it brought back the pain."

"I'm so sorry. I should have thought—"

Jack raised a hand to still her. He smiled. "Please, don't apologize. Along with the pain, he made me remember the joy. And somewhere in the last couple of days, Nate stopped being a reminder of Bobby and simply became Nate, a little person in his own right." He smiled. "Now, how do you like your coffee?"

"Black is fine."

"Let's take it out on the deck," he suggested.

She nodded and together they carried their coffee down the hallway and into his bedroom. As he opened the door to the deck, he tried not to look at the bed, tried not to imagine himself there with Marissa naked in his arms.

The night was warm, although a breeze from the water made it comfortable. The sky was brilliant with stars, illuminating the deck with a soft, silvery glow.

Marissa sat at the table and Jack eased down next to her. She looked lovely in the pale light and he could smell her sweet, floral scent riding on the salty breeze.

He took a sip of his coffee, then smiled at her. "It seems I've spent a lot of time the past couple of days thanking you, but I want to thank you again...for today, for the trip to Miami."

"I just hope something comes of it." She leaned forward and placed a hand on his arm. "It would be nice for me to know that you and Bobby are finally back together where you both belong."

He got up and moved to the railing. He stared out at the ocean waves, not willing to allow the hope her words offered to make its way into his heart. He sensed rather than saw her leave the table.

She moved to stand next to him, her gaze following his to the water. "It's so beautiful here," she said softly. "It must be lovely to watch a sunrise from here."

He turned to face her at the same time she turned to him. He didn't know if he took the first step toward her, or she moved toward him. He only knew that suddenly she was in his arms and he was drowning in the green of her eyes, and then he was drowning in the sweetness of her lips.

She didn't fight the kiss; rather, she leaned into him, as if she was as hungry, as needy as he felt.

He wrapped his arms around her, pulled her more intimately against him, felt the quickening of her breath against his mouth.

Splaying his hands across the small of her back, he deepened the kiss, their tongues dancing in a frantic rhythm of need.

The ocean breeze did nothing to cool the fever that had taken possession of Jack—it merely stoked his internal flames higher.

He moved his hands beneath her T-shirt, her back silky smooth beneath his palms. Still he held possession of her mouth, drinking her in, allowing the heat of her, the sweet of her to rush through him.

Finally, reluctantly, he broke the kiss and gazed at her, knowing his hunger shone from his eyes. "Stay with me, Marissa. Stay the night and watch the sunrise in the morning with me."

He saw her desire radiating from her eyes and once again his lips claimed hers with fiery intent. He couldn't remember ever wanting a woman as he now wanted Marissa. And he knew she wanted him with the same crazy intensity.

When he broke the kiss, they were both breathless. "Stay, Marissa," he whispered. He stroked the side of her face and she closed her eyes for a moment, as if finding his touch more than she could bear. "Let me make love to you, hold you in my arms. Stay the night, Marissa."

Chapter Nine

There was nothing that Marissa wanted to do more than to fall into the spell Jack wove with his words, his touch, his hungry kiss.

And for a moment she had allowed herself to fall gloriously into the passion he stirred in her. She had allowed herself to be swept into the flames of his kisses, the fire of his touch.

The night was set for romance, with the balmy light breeze that stirred sensually across her bare arms and legs. The stars overhead provided a backdrop of brilliant splendor and Jack's kisses were so hot she felt as if she were melting each time their mouths touched.

However, as she gazed into his eyes, so warm, so achingly blue, she recognized with horror that she wanted more than a night with Jack Coffey.

She wanted more than a night, more than a vacation of stirring memories. She wanted a lifetime with him. Somehow, some way, in the space of a mere week she had fallen in love with Jack Coffey.

She dropped her arms from around his neck and took a step backward, shocked by the realization that somehow, some way, Mr. Wrong had become her Mr. Right.

"Marissa?" Jack looked at her in confusion. "What's wrong?"

"Nothing...I..." She looked at him helplessly, staggered beyond words by the emotions that flowed through her. She loved Jack, loved him with all her heart. There was no mistaking what she felt.

"I've offended you...moved too fast." Jack cursed softly beneath his breath. "I'm sorry. I'm so out of practice. I—I thought you felt the same way I do. I thought you wanted me as much as I want you. Obviously I was mistaken."

"No, you aren't mistaken." She raised a trembling hand to her pounding heart. "I want you, Jack. There's nothing I'd like more than to fall into bed with you. I want you as I've never wanted before."

"Then I don't understand..."

"I know you don't." Marissa felt the need to run, escape, before she made an utter fool of herself. How could this have happened? How had Jack crawled so completely into her heart, her soul? She turned and left the deck.

He caught up with her before she could leave his

bedroom. He took her by the arm, stopping her forward progress and forcing her back to face him.

"Marissa, wait. Make me understand." His gaze played over her features, searching for answers.

Marissa's gaze fell to his bed. The navy spread was slightly rumpled and one of the pillows still held the faint indentation from his head.

The sheets would smell of him, and for a moment her mind exploded with a vision of her and Jack beneath those sheets, their bodies naked and moving together. They would be good together. She knew their lovemaking would be something stupendous.

She wished desperately that she could simply fall into that bed with him, forget any desire for a future and just enjoy the moment of splendid passion. But she couldn't.

With an effort, she pulled her gaze away from the bed and back to Jack. She drew a deep breath, fighting the emotion that suddenly burned at her eyes, thickened in her throat. "I can't stay the night. I can't make love with you, because I want to so badly, it hurts inside me. Because it's already going to be too hard to forget you."

Suddenly Marissa was angry, not angry at Jack, not necessarily angry with herself, but angry with fate. "It wasn't supposed to be this way," she exclaimed. "It wasn't supposed to be at all like this."

Jack eyed her helplessly, bewilderment shining from his eyes. "What are you talking about? What wasn't supposed to be this way?"

"It was supposed to be right this time. I was supposed to know the instant I met him. I'd know and he'd know and it would be the beginning of something lasting and wonderful." She knew she was rambling, but she couldn't stop herself.

The words spilled out of her, tumbling one after another. "It's not fair. You snuck up on me, Jack. I didn't even think I liked you at first. And now I've gone and fallen in love with you."

There, she'd said it. And someplace deep inside her, she'd been hoping that once she said the words, he would sweep her into his arms and profess his undying love for her.

But that didn't happen. Instead, he stared at her with more than a little disbelief and a touch of distinct horror. "Marissa, I—I don't know what to say," he finally said.

Any tiny bit of hope that might have flourished in her heart quickly died a painful death. "And that pretty well says it all."

She left the bedroom and walked down the hallway, Jack hurrying behind her. "Marissa, surely you're mistaken," he said. "I know we've spent a lot of time together, and maybe you're just lonely and I'm just convenient."

She turned to face him when they reached the living room. "I wish I were mistaken. But this isn't about me being lonely. This isn't about vacation madness." She swallowed hard. "Jack, I'm in love with you."

"But we've only known each other for a week."

"I know," she agreed. Along with her hope, her anger fled, leaving her only confused and exhausted. "It's crazy. You're nothing like my Mr. Right."

"I'm crabby."

She nodded. "And stubborn."

"I don't pick up after myself."

"You're a complete slob, and I can't explain why I love you. You are the last person in the world I would have chosen for myself. But it's happened." Her voice held the utter certainty of her feelings.

His gaze studied her for a long moment, and in the depths of his eyes she thought she saw a battle being waged, a battle she didn't understand. "It could never work," he finally said.

And in those words, hope renewed itself in Marissa. "What could never work?" she asked, her heart pounding frantically.

"Us. Any kind of a future for us." He said the words slowly, thoughtfully, and as he gazed at her, Marissa saw a softness, a tenderness in his eyes that strengthened her hope.

Was it possible? Had he been taken by surprise, too? Was it possible he'd fallen in love with her? She took a step toward him, wondering if he could hear the beat of her heart, the intense yearning that soared through every vein, filled every fiber of her being.

"Jack?" She stood so close to him she could feel

his body heat. "Why couldn't we have a future to-gether? Because you don't love me?"

His eyes darkened and he refused to meet her gaze. "Because we're all wrong for each other."

He hadn't said he didn't love her. Joy suffused her. She knew Jack well enough to know that he wouldn't mince words, that if he didn't love her, he'd tell her in direct language. But he hadn't.

She reached up and cupped his face with her palms, forcing him to look her directly in the eyes. "Tell me again why we're wrong for each other. I seem to have forgotten."

Again a mixture of emotions flitted across his fea-tures, deepening the hue of his eyes. "Marissa." He pulled her hands off his face and took a step back. He raked a hand through his hair, his gaze once again not meeting hers. "I think we're mistaking lust for love here."

"No. I know the difference between lust and love," she protested. "I know that I want you, that I want you to kiss me until my head spins, caress me until I can't think. I know I lust for you. But I also know I want to share your laughter, I want to share your heartaches, I want to share your life. And that's not lust. It's love."

She thought she saw a spark of something in his eyes, but it was there only a moment, then gone. "Marissa, I can't be your Mr. Right. You told me yourself that your Mr. Right would have hopes and dreams. And I have neither. You deserve that in a man. You should demand that in a man.''

''But you aren't without hopes and dreams,'' she contradicted. She searched his features, loving the cleft in his chin, the faint five-o'clock shadow of whiskers, the way the color of his eyes reflected so accurately his mercurial moods.

At the moment his eyes were the deep blue of bewilderment and she wasn't sure if he was deliberately being obtuse or if he truly didn't see himself as the man he was.

''Oh, you had me fooled at first with all your cynical talk and crusty exterior, Jack.'' She stepped forward and took his hand, then led him down the hallway to Bobby's room.

She opened the door and with an effort pulled him into the little boy's room. ''Here is your hope, your dreams,'' she said softly.

He pulled his hands from hers, anger sparking in his eyes. ''You don't know what you're talking about.'' His voice gradually softened as he realized Nathaniel still slept soundly in the crib.

He stalked past her back to the living room and she quickly followed him. ''Jack, your hope lives in that room. A man who doesn't have hope or dreams in his heart doesn't keep a room like that. It isn't some unhealthy obsession that drives you to buy something for Bobby on his birthdays. It's hope.''

He walked to the window and stood, his back to Marissa. She held her breath, hoping her words had penetrated his thick skull, praying he recognized the man he was and not the man he professed to be.

When he turned back to face her, any light that had been in his eyes was gone and his features radiated a weary hopelessness that tore through her.

"That isn't hope." He pointed down the hallway in the direction of the bedroom. "That's atonement."

"Atonement? But that implies guilt. What on earth do you feel guilty about?"

Sheer torment radiated from him and Marissa fought against her impulse to go to him, embrace him and try to ease his pain. Instead she remained where she was, her need to comfort him aching inside her.

"I should have worked harder to love Sherry. Maybe then things would have been different. I should have worked harder, been good enough at my job to find Bobby." The words spewed from him, filled with self-loathing. "I don't know what I did, but it must have been something, for me to lose Bobby."

He drew a deep breath, as if in an attempt to tame the demons within. "Fate decided five years ago that I wasn't cut out to be a father."

"Fate didn't decide that," she exclaimed. "Sherry did. And you did everything you could to find Bobby. It wasn't your fault the woman you got in touch with was a flake."

He nodded, as if to concede the point, then sighed

wearily. "It really doesn't matter. Even if I were man enough to be with you, Nate deserves better than what I can give to him."

Marissa thought about her son, how easily, how quickly he'd taken to Jack, how naturally he'd called him Daddy.

"Nathaniel fell in love with you before I did," she said softly. "And you know what they say about small children and animals. They instinctively know the true nature of a person."

"It's no good, Marissa." There was a dreadful note of finality in his voice.

He walked to where she stood and touched the side of her face, a touch that ached inside her as she saw the dull lifelessness in his eyes.

"Go home, Marissa. Go back to Kansas City and find your Mr. Right. Find a man who can share your enthusiasm for life, your utter faith in love and happiness."

He dropped his hand from her face and turned away from her, leaving her feeling more bereft than she'd ever felt in her life.

The most difficult thing Jack had ever done in his life was to look into the vast green depths of Marissa's eyes, touch the silky skin on her face, then turn his back on her and all she was so openly offering him.

How had a fall on the beach transformed into such

an emotional mess? How had his simple, miserable life become so damned complicated?

He'd known from the very beginning that Marissa wasn't the kind of woman to be a ship passing in his night. He'd recognized the starry shine of belief in her eyes the moment he'd stumbled over her son. So, why hadn't he run for the hills at that very moment?

Because he couldn't run. Her son had broken his leg.

The humor of his thoughts did nothing to lift his spirits. He sensed Marissa behind him, felt her gaze on his back. He steeled his emotions, then turned back to face her.

He knew the luminous yearning in her eyes would haunt him for a very long time. But he also knew with certainty that he wasn't her Mr. Right, that he could never be the man she deserved.

"So that's it," she said. "You've decided to remain life's victim."

"No, I'm a realist, Marissa. And I'm not going to ruin your life by being a part of it."

She started to say something, then stopped and instead grabbed her purse from the sofa. "I'll just get Nathaniel and we'll be on our way." She turned and disappeared down the hallway.

Jack breathed a sigh of relief. If she'd stood there another minute, with those big eyes so filled with love, he might have done something stupid. He might have fallen into the fantasies, the dreams she spun.

She reappeared a moment later, Nathaniel snuggled against her, still fast asleep. ''Then I guess this is goodbye.''

''I guess so,'' he replied. For a long moment he stared at her, memorizing the features of her face...the dancing freckles across her nose, the stubborn thrust of her pointed chin, those beautiful eyes that shone so brightly.

If only she'd been content with passion, with lust. If only she'd been willing to fall into bed without commitments, without the messiness of emotions. Without the entanglement of love. Love, with its expectations. Expectations he could never fulfill.

''I hope things work out for you, Jack,'' she said softly as she moved toward the front door. ''I hope you find Bobby and the two of you build a beautiful life together.'' Before he could reply, she was gone.

For one crazy moment Jack wanted to race to the door and call her back inside. He fought against the impulse, knowing it would only lead to her eventual heartbreak.

Instead, he turned and went back to the deck, his head spinning with the knowledge that Marissa loved him. How was it possible? How on earth had it happened that a woman like her had fallen for a man like him?

Fate definitely had a sense of humor. A sick, pathetic sense of humor. And the sickest part of all was that Jack loved Marissa more than a little bit.

He closed his eyes and for a moment allowed that love to seep through him. He loved the way her skin felt beneath his fingertips, the silky softness of her halo of hair. But his love embraced more than the physical Marissa. He loved her wit, her humor, the gentleness of her spirit, the openness of her heart.

But if he followed his heart, if he allowed them to fall into a relationship, perhaps get married, how long would it be before she lost the optimism that guided her life? How long before her eyes lost their sparkle from the weight of living with his cynicism?

And what of Nathaniel? He deserved a father who was whole, a man with a complete and open heart. Jack had neither.

He stared out at the moonlit waves breaking onto the shore. No, it was better this way. He was meant to be alone. She was far better off without him. Eventually she would find her Mr. Right, a man who would believe as she believed, a man who could love Nathaniel without pain.

He frowned as he heard his own heartbeat, pounding a strange rhythm he'd never felt before. He finally recognized the rhythm as regret.

Chapter Ten

Marissa tried to enjoy the rest of her vacation, but two days after she'd walked out of Jack's house for good, she realized she couldn't.

The Florida sunshine reminded her of the heat of Jack's kisses, the blue sky overhead was reminiscent of his eyes. In the crashing ocean waves, she heard his voice, his heartbeat, and she knew she had to leave Mason Bridge, leave Florida and her vacation behind.

She needed to get back to work, to fill her days with enough work that she fell into bed at night too exhausted to dream.

Nathaniel was a mess, too, whiny and fussing, and she wondered if he somehow felt her heartache, perhaps missed Jack enough to have a little heartache of his own.

Three days after she'd left Jack's house, she and Nathaniel boarded a plane bound for home. Thankfully, Nathaniel fell asleep almost the minute the plane left the ground.

Marissa stared out the window, grief weighing heavy on her heart. The most difficult thing of all to accept was that Jack loved her but had chosen to turn his back on what was in his heart.

It would have been wonderful had her love been enough to heal the wounds left by Sherry and Bobby, but apparently his scars were too deep to be cured.

If only he'd been able to see that he was filled with the need to love and be loved, that believing in happiness wasn't a weakness or a fault, but rather a strength to be envied.

It was easy to believe in happy endings when everything was going well. The real test of faith was to believe in happy endings when things had gone so wrong.

The clouds outside the plane window blurred together as tears gathered in Marissa's eyes. She quickly swiped them away. She refused to cry over Jack Coffey. For the past three days she had managed not to cry, and she wasn't about to do so now.

She told herself Jack Coffey wasn't worth crying about. He was a man who had chosen the path of misery in his life and didn't warrant the emotion of her tears.

Her grandmother was waiting for them at the

Kansas City International Airport. At the sight of the trim, gray-haired woman, a burst of love filled Marissa. When Marissa's mother had died, Belle Wilson had put aside her own anguish over her daughter's death and opened her home and her heart to the two grief-stricken little girls. From that moment on, Belle had been a source of strength, of comfort and wisdom for Marissa.

"Ah, there are my darlings," she exclaimed as Marissa and Nathaniel came into view. She plucked Nathaniel from Marissa's arms and gave him a noisy kiss on the side of his face. Nathaniel giggled and wrapped his arms around his nana's neck.

"Are you okay?" She peered worriedly at Marissa.

"Fine." Marissa forced a wide smile. "We had a wonderful time," she said as they made their way toward the luggage carousel.

"If you had such a wonderful time, what are you doing home a week early?" Her grandmother's eyes peered into hers, as if to pierce her heart and see what lay within.

Marissa shrugged, her smile feeling stiff across her mouth. "We got tired of the rest and relaxation. We'd both had enough of the beach and I was just ready to come home."

Belle stared at Marissa for another long moment, then sniffed in disbelief. "I suppose you'll tell me what happened when you're ready."

"There's nothing to tell," Marissa protested, but her words sounded false even to her own ears.

It took nearly twenty minutes for them to collect the luggage and get settled in Belle's car. Finally they were on their way to Marissa's small house.

As they zoomed down the interstate that would take them to the north suburb where Marissa lived, thoughts of Jack once again played in her mind.

What was he doing at this very moment? Did he miss her at all? Had she touched him in any way? And the biggest question of all—how long would it take for her to finally forget him? Would she ever be able to forget him?

"So, you want to talk about it?" Belle broke the silence that had fallen in the car.

"What makes you so sure there's anything to talk about?"

Belle smiled. "I know my girl, and I see shadows in those eyes that weren't there when you left here."

Marissa stared out the window, unsure if she was ready to talk about Jack. Even his name evoked an incredible pain inside her.

She turned to look at Belle. "When you met Grandpa, was it love at first sight?"

"Oh, my heavens, no." Belle laughed. "When I met your grandpa, I thought he was the most arrogant, obnoxious man I'd ever known." Her laughter faded to a soft smile. "But by our third date I knew I wanted him in my life forever."

Marissa frowned thoughtfully. "I always believed

when I met the man who was right for me, I'd know it in an instant and that it would be mutual.''

"That's a nice fantasy, but if that were true, we wouldn't have songs about broken hearts and unrequited love.''

Marissa sighed. "I guess that's true.''

"So, is that what this is about—a broken heart?'' Belle asked softly. Tears burned at Marissa's eyes and she nodded her head. "Some good-looking beach bum took advantage of you?''

"No, nothing like that.'' A small smile curved Marissa's lips. "Actually, Nathaniel broke his leg.''

"What?'' Belle wheeled into the driveway of the rental house where Marissa lived. "Wait. Let's get inside, then I want to hear everything.''

Fifteen minutes later, with Nathaniel sitting happily in his familiar high chair and with fresh coffee in front of the adults, Marissa found herself telling Belle about Jack.

She told her of their ill-fated first meeting and of Jack's injuries, of their subsequent time spent together and about Jack's past.

Marissa had hoped that by talking it out, she'd see how crazy it was that she'd fallen in love with Jack so quickly, so devastatingly. But talking about it didn't ease the pain; rather, it made the ache sharper, more intense.

"I know it's crazy,'' she said to Belle. "I only knew him such a short time.''

Belle smiled softly. "Love doesn't know time.

Love can happen in the flash of an eye, the beat of a heart, or it can grow slowly over years of shared experiences and time.''

"The most difficult thing of all to accept is that I know Jack was falling in love with me." Marissa paused a moment, remembering their kisses, the tenderness in his eyes at odd moments when they'd been together. "But he was afraid to trust in it. He was so afraid to believe in love."

Belle reached over and patted Marissa's hand. "Honey, you know what they say about a sow's ear and a silk purse. The same is certainly true with this Jack. You can't make a believer out of one who has lost all faith."

Marissa nodded. She knew what her grandmother said was true. And she told herself she was better off without Jack in her life. Still, she desperately wished her heart would listen to her head.

For four days Jack prowled the confines of his house like a prisoner on house arrest, his mood worse than a grizzly bear whose winter sleep had been disturbed.

He knew with certainty that he'd done the right thing in sending Marissa and Nathaniel away, but he couldn't get the regret out of his head, out of his heart.

Even though he had sent her away, she remained in every room of the house. The sound of her laughter rang in his ears as he poured himself morning coffee. The vision of her animated face danced before his eyes as he made his lunch. He imagined he smelled the scent of her as he tossed and turned in bed each night.

And it wasn't just Marissa who haunted him. It was Nathaniel, as well. The little boy's big blue eyes and delightful grin refused to vacate Jack's memory.

When they had been on the stakeout and Jack had held Nate in his lap while the toddler slept, Jack had been filled with a kind of quiet peace he hadn't felt since he'd held Bobby as a little boy.

He now stood on his deck, a cup of coffee in hand as he watched the morning sunlight dance atop the breaking waves. Even here, in the sunshine and salty air, Nate's and Marissa's shadows lingered, filling him with an abiding loneliness he'd never before experienced.

He could never get back the lost years with Bobby. Even if Barbara Klein called him tomorrow and managed to somehow arrange a reunion between himself and his son, the past five years would forever be lost.

It was odd, really, that Nate was about the age Bobby had been when Sherry had taken him away. It was almost as if fate were giving Jack a second chance to parent a needy child.

And Marissa. She wasn't a second chance at love. She was the first woman he'd cared about with such depth, with such emotion...with love.

He sipped his coffee and watched a gull dive into

the water, then a second later soar into the sky. That was what Marissa had done to him. She had plucked him from the depths of his misery and cast him into the uncertain air where hope had teased him, where dreams could reach him.

And it had scared the hell out of him. Life's victim or life's survivor? The question she'd asked him whirled in his head.

He turned as he heard the ringing of his doorbell. He limped toward the door and opened it to Maria. "It's not your cleaning day today, is it?" he asked with a frown.

"No, but I came to tell you I can't clean for you next week." Maria swept past him, her broad features beaming with happiness.

"Why not?" Jack followed her.

Maria lowered herself onto the sofa with all the grace of a regal queen. "Next week my husband and I will be enjoying a Caribbean cruise."

Jack sank into the chair across from her and eyed her in disbelief. "Maria, I've told you before, those promotional flyers you get in the mail for cheap cruises are scams."

"This is no scam, Jack." Her eyes sparkled with suppressed excitement. She leaned forward. "It finally happened."

"What finally happened?" he asked in bewilderment.

"The Lotto." She squealed and pulled a Lotto ticket out of her purse. "I always knew someday I'd hit, and it finally happened. Five numbers out of six. Ten thousand dollars!'' She jumped up from the sofa and danced a happy jig.

Despite his black mood, Jack found himself laughing. Her excitement was infectious, and Jack knew there was nobody who could use the good fortune as much as Maria and her husband.

He stood and gave her a quick hug. ''I'm happy for you, Maria.''

She shrugged. ''It's not a fortune, but it'll help some. And when we get back from the cruise, I'll clean this place one time for free.''

''You don't have to do that,'' Jack protested as they walked back toward the front door. ''I pay you what you're worth. Actually, I pay you more than you're worth,'' he teased.

Maria laughed, then sobered and eyed him seriously. ''She's good for you, Jack. The shadows in your eyes have eased. She and that little boy— they're your winning Lotto ticket.''

Jack didn't bother to tell her that he'd been a fool and had thrown away his winning ticket. As Maria waved goodbye and stepped out his door, regret once again surged inside him.

Visions of Marissa and Nate swept through his mind, filling him with a deep, abiding yearning for what might have been.

Victim or survivor? Marissa's words echoed in his ears.

Would he forever mourn what might have been

and not reach out to embrace what might be in his future? Would he allow his memories to obstruct any hope for happiness in the future?

His misery had held a certain comfort in that it was familiar, without surprises. Now the misery that swept through him as he thought of life without Marissa only felt...miserable.

He was the only one who could decide his role in life. Only he was in control of his future, and he had to decide if he wanted to remain alone with his memories or build a future with the woman and child he loved.

Energy soared through him, an energy intensified by the greatest need he'd ever known and an undercurrent of fear that he'd come to his senses too late.

He moved as quickly as he could to the front door, adrenaline sizzling through him. He opened the door and leaned over the stair railing. "Maria! Maria!"

She had reached her car, and now peered up at him.

"I need you to do me a favor," he said.

She grinned. "It's going to cost you."

He laughed, feeling more free than he had in days. "Trust me, it's worth whatever it costs."

"Mr. Johnson in room 241 wants you to look in on him," Roberta Stamm, the head nurse, said to

Marissa. "I know you were ready to go home, but could you check on him before you go?"

"Of course," Marissa replied, and took off down the hospital hallway for room 241. This was her first day back to work. Her grandmother had tried to talk her into taking the full three weeks off, but Marissa had wanted to come back to work immediately upon returning from Mason Bridge.

She needed to be around people who had genuine illness, people who needed her comfort, her expertise, so she wouldn't be so focused on her own broken heart. She needed to be busy so she couldn't think about Jack Coffey.

And the day had been incredibly busy. Unfortunately she'd discovered that no matter what her task, no matter how hard she concentrated on a chore, thoughts of Jack intruded.

She entered room 241 and gave the gray-haired man a wide smile. "Hi, Mr. Johnson. Nurse Stamm said you wanted to see me."

'I'd rather be seeing the four walls of my own house," the man said grumpily.

"It won't be long and you'll be able to go home," Marissa soothed. Mr. Johnson had suffered a nasty case of pneumonia, but was now on the mend. "Now, what can I do for you?"

"You plumped my pillows real nice this morning and I wanted you to plump them again." He sat up, indicating the flattened pillows behind his head.

"I think I can handle that." Marissa picked up

one of the pillows and plumped it in her arms, then did the same with the other. She replaced them on the bed. "There, see if that's better."

Mr. Johnson leaned back and closed his eyes. "Much better." He opened his eyes and offered her a shy smile.

"I'm going home now, Mr. Johnson, but Polly Manson will be on duty and she's an absolutely wonderful pillow plumper."

He nodded. "Have a good night." He frowned again. "Wish I were going home."

She laughed. "You'll be home before you know it." With a goodbye, Marissa left the room and headed for the nurses' station, where she retrieved her purse and signed out.

Already she dreaded the night to come. Nathaniel had been unusually fussy since they'd come back from their trip. If she didn't know better, she'd think he missed Jack as much as she did.

"Marissa Criswell to the ER waiting area *stat*."

Marissa froze. For a moment, the male voice booming over the hospital's intercom system had sounded remarkably like Jack's. But that was impossible. Jack was in Florida. Jack had sent her and her love away from him.

She hurried to the elevator that would take her downstairs to the ER, wondering if she was going to be asked to pull a double shift. Although she usually tried to accommodate when the hospital was short staffed, there was no way she intended to work another shift tonight.

Since coming back from Florida, she'd been uncharacteristically tired and she knew deep inside her heart that it was a weariness born of depression. She missed Jack.

Time, she reminded herself. Only time would heal the heart he'd broken.

She heard the sound of raised voices before she entered the waiting-room area.

"Sir, you cannot use the intercom system for your own personal purposes." Marissa recognized the voice of Nancy Noland, one of the ER nurses.

"This is a matter of life and death. Stop being so stingy and let me use that microphone again."

Marissa froze just outside the door that would lead her into the waiting area. Jack. Nobody else had that deep tone of exasperation. Nobody else sounded quite so cranky.

What was he doing here? Why had he come? She refused to second-guess him—he was too perverse for that.

She drew a deep, trembling breath, then pushed open the door, and there he stood at the nurses' station. Jack. His leg was still in a cast, his fingers still wrapped and he wore a mutinous expression of determination.

"Look, just let me call her one more time," he said.

A red stain of frustration colored Nancy's face

and she shook her head. "Why don't you just take a seat and relax."

"I can't relax," Jack growled.

"Jack?" Marissa said softly, and she wasn't sure who was happier to see her, Jack or Nancy.

"Marissa, thank God." He advanced toward her, and Marissa was vaguely aware of the two of them garnering the interest of the others in the waiting room.

"Wha-what are you doing here?" she asked, the very sight of him ripping a new hole in her heart.

Jack scowled at the people around him, then looked back at Marissa. "Do you have any idea how many hospitals there are in Kansas City?" he asked.

"Not off the top of my head," she replied, still reeling with the shock of finding him here.

"There's a bunch, and I spent all day yesterday and most of today trying to find the one where you work."

"How did you get here?"

"I got Maria to take me to the airport, caught a flight, and since arriving here in Kansas City I've aggravated a dozen taxi drivers trying to find you."

"But why?" Marissa wasn't about to hope. She wasn't about to try to anticipate the reason for Jack's presence. Maybe he was here on a case and just wanted to stop by and say hello.

He glared at the people who all appeared quite interested in their conversation. Grabbing Marissa's arm, he pulled her out the door and into the late-afternoon sunshine. He eyed her for a long moment before he finally spoke. "When you left, you took something from me."

She stared at him in disbelief. Did he think she'd stolen something from him? Outrage swept through her. And he was just stubborn enough to hunt her down like a criminal. "And what exactly do you think I took? A suitcase full of fast-food wrappers?" she snapped.

His dark eyebrows rose in surprise and he laughed. His laughter wrapped around Marissa. He swept a hand through his hair, leaving it in charming disarray. "I'm bungling this badly." He took her hand in his, all laughter gone from his beautiful blue eyes. "Marissa, I wanted you to be a ship in the night, passing through my life without rippling the waters."

"I know." His hand around Marissa's sent warmth shooting up her arm.

He released her hand and once again raked it through his hair. "You rippled the waters. God, but you did ripple my life. And when you left, you took my disbelief, my cynicism, my very heart with you."

For the first time since seeing him, Marissa allowed a tiny touch of hope to fill her.

He moved restlessly, as if unable to stand still. "Victim or survivor? That's what you asked me the last night we were together. I've been a victim for the last five years. I'm not anymore. Somehow I've become a survivor who has lived through hell and come out on the other side believing that happiness is possible, love is possible...we are possible.'' He had to yell the last words in order to be heard above the ambulance that had pulled in next to where they stood.

''We?'' she echoed faintly. Had she heard him correctly? She stared at him as he continued to speak, but whatever he was saying was lost beneath the blare of the siren.

He stopped talking and the ambulance parked and the siren went silent. Together Marissa and Jack watched as the two EMTs pulled out a stretcher bearing a frail, gray-haired woman.

''I told him it was just gas pains, not my heart, but he didn't listen to me,'' she said as they unloaded her. ''He never listens to me.''

Jack turned back to Marissa. ''Marry me.''

She stared at him in astonishment. ''Pardon me?'' She wondered if the noise of the siren had damaged her ears. She could have sworn he'd just asked her to marry him.

The old woman on the stretcher looked from Jack to Marissa. ''If you love him, honey, better say yes fast. Life is short and before you know it you're at the hospital all because you ate a burrito with chili.'' Before she could say anything more, the EMTs wheeled her through the doors and into the emergency room.

Marissa turned to look at Jack once again, her

head reeling. He didn't give her a chance to speak a word. Rather, he gathered her in his arms and she could feel the beat of his heart against her own.

"I knew you were trouble the moment I saw you standing over me," he said, his voice husky. "Those blond curls of yours were gleaming in the sunshine, and seeing you in that blue bikini made me momentarily forget my pain. I love you, Marissa. I want you...need you in my life. Marry me. For God's sake, will you please marry me?" He was naked before her, vulnerability in the depths of his beautiful eyes.

The hope she had desperately tried to tamp down, afraid that it might be false, now blossomed inside her. He'd said he loved her. The words sang through her veins, rang in her heart. But still, she hesitated.

With enormous reluctance, she stepped out of his embrace. "Before I answer your question, I need to know something, Jack." Her insides trembled with the importance of her question. As much as she loved Jack, she would sacrifice that love if his answer wasn't right.

The sunshine that had seemed so warm only moments before now seemed cooler as she faced him. "I have to know that you have the ability to love Nathaniel, that your love will be for him as the little boy he is, and not as a replacement for Bobby." Tears blurred her eyes. "He can't be the child you lost, Jack. It would be too big a burden for him."

Jack smiled, a tender smile that shot a welcoming

warmth through her. He reached out and stroked her cheek with a finger.

"I have to be honest with you, Marissa. There will always be a space in my heart that belongs to Bobby. But I have a huge heart, and there's room enough for one special little terminator who literally and figuratively knocked me off my feet. I love Nate and I love you."

For a moment Marissa couldn't reply. Tears of joy seeped from her eyes and filled her throat. She laughed and threw herself into his arms.

"Hey," the little gray-haired woman who had come in on the ambulance called out when the ER doors opened. "I've got to know. Are you going to marry him?"

Jack's arms tightened around Marissa, as if he were afraid of what she might say. She looked into his eyes...the eyes of the man she loved, the beautiful eyes of the man who was every fantasy she'd ever entertained. "Yes," she replied. "Yes, I'm going to marry him."

Before she could say another word, his lips crashed down to hers.

The kiss was filled with intense passion, with enduring love and all its endless possibilities and dreams. The kiss wrapped warmth not only around her, but inside her, filling her up as if she'd swallowed the sun. And she knew the rightness of this moment, and this man, and her future.

By the time they broke the kiss, the old lady had

disappeared back behind the doors. Marissa reached up and placed a palm against his cheek. "I still can't believe how the man I believed was Mr. Wrong became Mr. Right."

Again he smiled, his eyes lit with love. "It doesn't matter, does it? The important thing is that I'm your Mr. Right, and you're my Mrs. Right and we're going to spend the rest of our lives living happily ever after."

Again their lips met in a kiss. "Speaking of the terminator," Jack said when the kiss ended. "Where is he?"

"At the day care center." Marissa looked at her watch. "I need to pick him up."

"Then let's go," Jack replied. They walked to Marissa's car and got in. "I know you probably think I'm crazy, but I still think that first morning on the beach, I didn't just trip over Nate. I think he tripped me on purpose."

Marissa smiled. "If that's really true, then maybe we should thank him. If he hadn't tripped you up, you would have just been a jogger running by me on the beach."

Jack leaned over and kissed her on the neck. "Yeah, remind me to buy Nate a fantastic birthday present."

Shivers of pleasure swept through Marissa. "I think the best present you're giving him is yourself."

He sat back and looked at her, obviously touched

by her words. "I love you," he said, then grinned. "And you were worth a broken leg. Now, let's go get our son."

Marissa pulled away from the hospital, pointed in the direction of her happily-ever-after.

Nathaniel was depressed. He'd been depressed since they had left Florida, but today was the worst day of all because he'd had to face obnoxious Claire and Julie at the Hickory Dickory Day Care.

All day they'd been teasing him because he'd come home as fatherless as when he'd left. He'd spent most of the day in a corner, quietly playing by himself and ignoring the two tormentors.

He didn't understand it. He'd done everything possible to make Jack his dad. He knew his mom had liked Jack, and he'd thought Jack liked his mom. He didn't understand how grown-ups could mess things up so badly.

Tonight his mommy would be as sad as he was. She tried to hide it, but he knew she was sad. She missed Daddy Jack, and so did he.

He put a blue block on top of a red one and wondered if he'd have time to build something before his mommy came to pick him up.

"Hey, Nate."

The voice was deep, familiar. Nathaniel looked up and saw Daddy Jack and his mother standing with Miss Samantha at the door to the day care.

Nathaniel struggled to his feet, happiness soaring

through him...happiness better than a red lollipop, better than a new truck with shiny wheels.

"Daddy?" He took a step toward Jack, saw the smile on his mommy's face and knew his dream was coming true. Jack opened his arms and Nathaniel raced toward him.

Suddenly he was in big strong arms that lifted him up high. "Daddy!" Nathaniel squealed in delight.

"That's right, kiddo. I'm gonna be your daddy for ever and always," Jack said.

Nathaniel threw his arms around his daddy's neck, his mind whirling with all the wonderful things they would share. Daddy threw an arm around Mommy's shoulders. "Come on, let's go plan our future."

As his daddy carried him toward the door, Nathaniel gazed over his shoulder at Julie and Claire, who watched in astonishment.

He grinned, then waved happily as his daddy carried him out of the day care.

Epilogue

"Are you sure I look okay?" Jack asked Marissa.

"Honey, for the third time, you look wonderful." She smiled at him and patted the chair next to her. "Come and sit down and try to relax. Mrs. Klein said it would be a few minutes."

Jack eased into the chair next to her, trying to still the frantic beat of his heart. They were in a conference room in Miami, where in mere minutes Jack would see his son, Bobby, for the first time in years.

It had taken three months of dealing with red tape, sloughing through bureaucratic nonsense and filling out form after form, but finally the day Jack had never thought would happen was happening.

"What if he doesn't like me?" Jack asked softly, and turned to look at Marissa.

She smiled and took his hand in hers. "He's going to love you, just like I do. Just like Nathaniel does."

Jack squeezed her hand and closed his eyes, for a moment overcome with emotion too great to handle.

He and Marissa had married a month before and settled into life together in Mason Bridge. She had gotten a job in Edmund Hall's doctor office and Jack had gone back to the police force. Every day for Jack was like a gift as he discovered the depth of his love for his wife, and the amazing fact that she loved him back.

He looked over to Nate, who had found the toy box at the end of the room and was busily digging through the contents. Nate was a bonus gift that fate had given to him, and the bond between the little boy and Jack had become something shining and strong.

He stood, too nervous to remain seated, and began to pace the area in front of the chairs. What if Sherry, before her death, had told Bobby he was a bad man? What if Bobby wanted nothing to do with him?

All Jack wanted was an opportunity to love his son, an opportunity to be a good father to him. He hoped...he prayed that they hadn't come this far only to be disappointed.

The door opened and Barbara Klein entered. Following just behind her was a dark-haired, brown-eyed boy. Jack's heart seemed to pause in its beating as he laid eyes on his son.

"Bobby, this is the man I was telling you about," Barbara Klein said. "This is Jack Coffey."

"Hi." Bobby offered Jack a shy smile and Jack fought the impulse to scoop up the boy and squeeze him in his arms, to hold him so tightly nothing and nobody would ever part them again.

"Hi," Jack replied, fighting an emotion so intense it threatened to swallow him up. Hungrily, he gazed at Bobby, memorizing each and every feature.

"I'm going to go grab a cup of coffee," Barbara said.

"Would you mind if Nathaniel and I join you?" Marissa asked, and stood. Jack looked at her in panic. She smiled. "You need some time alone with your son," she said softly.

In her words he recognized the truth and he loved her all the more for knowing what he needed and allowing him some time alone with the child he had lost…and now found.

A moment later Marissa, Barbara and Nate were gone, leaving Jack alone with Bobby. "You want to sit?" he asked, and gestured to the chairs.

Bobby shrugged. "Okay." He sat in one of the chairs and Jack sat next to him.

"Did Mrs. Klein tell you who I am?" Jack asked.

Bobby nodded. "She said you're my biological dad."

Biological dad. That sounded so cold, so impersonal. "Yeah, I'm your biological dad and I've been looking for you, praying to find you, for the last five years."

"You have?" Bobby's brown eyes met his, and in his son's eyes he saw suspicion and confused uncertainty.

"Indeed I have." Jack placed an arm around the back of Bobby's chair, careful not to touch him, but leaning closer so he could smell the little-boy scent of him, so achingly familiar. "There's been a room for you at my house for all these years. Every year on your birthday I'd buy you a present, and at Christmastime I'd buy you what I thought you might want if you were with me."

"You did?" The suspicion was still in his eyes. "Where do you live?"

"In a little town about five hours from here called Mason Bridge. My house is right on the beach and when you were little, I'd sit on my deck and rock you, and the sound of the waves would put you to sleep."

Bobby frowned thoughtfully. "I think I remember that."

Jack wanted desperately to wrap his arms around his son, feel his warmth. But he also knew gaining Bobby's trust would take time, and that he'd have to earn Bobby's love.

"That woman who was in here with you. Is she your wife?"

"Yes, and she has a son named Nate. He's two years old."

Bobby thought for a moment. "And we're all going to live in the same house?"

"That's right," Jack said. "Bobby, I know this is all pretty overwhelming at the moment. But I'll tell you this. I love you. I've loved you every day of your life. And if you'll give us a chance, I think we'll be all right together. Will you give us a chance?"

He held his breath, afraid of the days, weeks, years lost. Was it too late? He knew that to a child, a day could feel like a lifetime. Had too many lifetimes gone by for Bobby?

Bobby looked at him, and beneath the doubts, beyond the self-protection, Jack saw a glimmer of need, and in that need Jack saw hope. Time and love—Jack knew those were the ingredients that would take away the suspicions, the defensive shell Bobby had grown for protection. Time and love, and Jack had plenty of both.

"What do you say? You'll give us a chance?" Jack held out his hand.

Bobby sat stone still for a long moment, then he slid his hand into Jack's for a firm handshake. "Okay."

Jack felt as if the world had momentarily stopped whirling, and had only restarted the moment Bobby spoke his assent.

A minute later he and Bobby left the conference

room and saw Marissa and Nate sitting in the waiting room. Marissa stood, a worried frown creasing her forehead, and Jack had never loved her more than he did at this moment.

She was the keeper of his dreams, his heart, his soul, and he smiled at her and saw her frown fall away.

"Bobby is ready for all of us to go home now," Jack said.

Marissa's eyes clouded with tears of joy. "That's wonderful."

At that moment Nate walked over to Bobby and threw his arms around him. "Bubbie," Nate exclaimed, and grinned at Marissa and Jack.

"I think that means Nathaniel is going to like having you for a brother," Marissa said.

Nate laughed and clapped his hands, pleased that his mother had understood. A big brother! It was the most awesome thing that had ever happened to him, other than getting Daddy Jack to be his daddy.

As the four of them walked toward the car, Nate grabbed hold of Bobby's hand and offered him his most charming smile. He could tell Bobby was a little bit nervous and he wished he could tell him that everything was going to be just fine. But Nate didn't have the grown-up words that he needed yet. So he did the next best thing—he offered Bobby his biggest grin.

Bobby smiled, just a little one, but it was enough. Nate knew it wouldn't take long and Bobby would find out that Daddy Jack was the very best daddy in the world, and Mommy was the very best mommy in the world. And Nate intended to be the most awesome little brother Bobby could ever wish for.

He laughed out loud. Oh, yes, life was good. He'd not only got the daddy he'd always wanted, but he'd got something even better. A family.

* * * * *

Don't miss Carla Cassidy's
next book from Silhouette Romance,
available in April.

#1 *New York Times* bestselling author

Nora Roberts

brings you more of the loyal and loving,
tempestuous and tantalizing Stanislaski family.

Coming in February 2001

The Stanislaski Sisters

Natasha and Rachel

Though raised in the Old World traditions of their
family, fiery Natasha Stanislaski and cool, classy
Rachel Stanislaski are ready for a *new* world of love....

*And also available in February 2001 from
Silhouette Special Edition, the newest book in the
heartwarming Stanislaski saga*

CONSIDERING KATE

Natasha and Spencer Kimball's daughter Kate turns her
back on old dreams and returns to her hometown, where
she finds the *man* of her dreams.

Available at your favorite retail outlet.

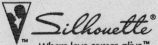

Where love comes alive™

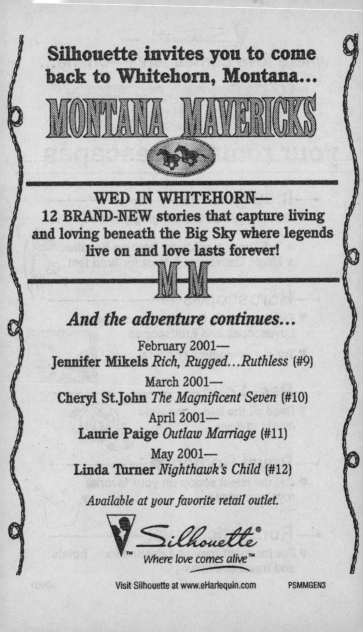

Coming in January 2001 from Silhouette Books...

ChildFinders, Inc.:
An Uncommon Hero

by

MARIE FERRARELLA

the latest installment of this bestselling author's popular miniseries.

The assignment seemed straightforward: track down the woman who had stolen a boy and return him to his father. But ChildFinders, Inc. had been duped, and Ben Underwood soon discovered that nothing about the case was as it seemed. Gina Wassel, the supposed kidnapper, was everything Ben had dreamed of in a woman, and suddenly he had to untangle the truth from the lies—before it was too late.

Available at your favorite retail outlet.